BUGLE BOY

MEMORIES

"Life is like a bugle call — full of high notes,
low notes and sometimes, flat notes."

Roy Goostrey

Order this book online at www.trafford.com
or email orders@trafford.com

Most Trafford titles are also available at major online book retailers.

Bugle Boy

Note for Librarians: A cataloguing record for this book is available from Library
and Archives Canada at www.collectionscanada.ca/amicus/index-e.html

Printed in Victoria, BC, Canada.

ISBN: 978-1-4269-1676-2 (sc)
ISBN: 978-1-4269-1677-9 (dj)

Library of Congress Control Number: 2009936087

*Our mission is to efficiently provide the world's finest, most comprehensive
book publishing service, enabling every author to experience success.
To find out how to publish your book, your way, and have it available
worldwide, visit us online at www.trafford.com*

Trafford rev. 11/13/2009

 www.trafford.com

North America & international
toll-free: 1 888 232 4444 (USA & Canada)
phone: 250 383 6864 ♦ fax: 812 355 4082

FOREWORD

MEMOIRS ARE WRITTEN BY a storyteller drawing us into his life experiences and painting pictures of times and places others have never been. These stories are generated by the questions our children often ask: "Where did you go to school, Grandfather?" "Dad, when did you first meet Mom?" "What was it like in the war years?" These questions, posed by our children and grandchildren, need to be answered before we die, or the answers will be lost forever.

I have presented the material in a clear, concise format, which encourages the reader to follow me through the seventy-five years of my life.

This work is dedicated to my three sons and my grandchildren, and in memory of Patricia, who passed away before she was able to see them nurture and grow into the wonderful family she would have been proud of.

ACKNOWLEDGEMENTS

WHILE THE DETAILS PRESENTED are descriptions of my own experiences, I wish to acknowledge the extensive editing and suggestions constantly available and honestly given by my wife, Yvonne. I learned much from her ongoing desire to ensure this material was meaningful and entertaining.

I was able to turn to my sister Audrey, my brother-in-law Alban, and my friends, John and Maureen Bell, who reminded me of forgotten, but important, details. I also include a long-lost schoolboy friend, Peter Yarwood, for his humourous and extensive reminders of the past.

Chapter 1

CARNIVAL DAY

In July 1946, on the day of the Stockport Carnival, I nearly lost my life. I was twelve years old.

The Stockport Carnival parade, an annual event since the late 1920's, had survived the Great Depression. This parade was special because World War II was over, and peace had been declared; everyone looked forward to happier times.

Living in an industrial town, surrounded by gas works, railway shunting yards, cotton and woolen mills, soot and grime, it was a rare pleasure for us to see the sun shining as it did on this special day. Since early morning, excited onlookers were placing boxes, benches and chairs along the edge of the pavement, waiting for the parade to start. The clowns and street vendors were already selling their wares — flags, balloons, and streamers to wave when the parade passed by.

As the morning progressed, many bands and dance troupes, walkers in fancy costumes, decorated wagons and lorries and buses continued to move up Great Portwood Street toward St. Paul's Church, the assembling point for all the participants. My excitement grew as the time wore on, but I knew that before I could watch the parade I had to rush down to the mill to take my Uncle Joe his lunch. If I hurried, I could get back in time to see the parade starting at 1:00 p.m.

It may have been Saturday, but the cotton mills and woolen mills were fully operational so that not everyone would be able to see the parade. I grabbed the lunch and ran toward the mill, followed by my cousin George, Uncle Joe's eight-year-old son, who had pestered me into coming along to help deliver the lunch.

We hurried down the street, past the houses, past the high brick wall wall that surrounded the railway shunting yards, and finally ran under the railway bridge where the street opened up into a meadow. There stood the Meadow Mill, as well as other mills, factories and houses in the surrounding area, which were built during the Industrial Revolution. Over time, smoke and grime dulled most of the original red brick walls so that only in a few places, protected from the elements, could the original colour be seen.

The property housing the mill was enclosed by a fence consisting of large stone pillars supporting wrought-iron railings, which ran several feet high and which were secured together to form a continuous wall between the pillars. The only breaks in this stone wall were the large, ornate, wrought-iron gates at the front and the rear entrances to the mill. One of the sections of railings, which had become disconnected from its bolts and had been temporarily secured by twisted wire, could be swung open to serve as an additional gate. The river Tame ran close by the mill and, while we waited for Uncle Joe to come to meet us, we skipped stones across the water.

Soon we became bored, and with nothing else to do but wait, I leaned back on the railings, only to feel them move. I tried pulling away quickly but not before that section of iron railings came crashing down upon me, the weight pinning me to the ground. Lying beneath the railings, I felt an excruciating pain throbbing in my head, my eyesight went fuzzy and I could taste the blood that had run from my nose into my mouth. After trying to raise the railing section off me, George ran away screaming for help. Uncle Joe, who came hurrying to the scene with fellow workers, shouted, "Go get his mother!"

I lay there, for what seemed an eternity, before I heard the sound of several people running toward me, and someone shouting orders to lift the iron railings off me. The hospital had been alerted, because I heard in the distance the growing sound of the ambulance siren, which stopped when it reached my side. An attendant had applied bandages to my head before my anxious mother arrived on the scene. I was placed on a stretcher and lifted into the ambulance. During the journey to the hospital, I kept gagging from the blood in my mouth so that the attendant had to remove the bandage from around my face to allow me to breathe. When I arrived at the hospital, I was rushed into emergency and quickly attended to by the doctor and nurses. They cleaned and dressed my visible injuries and took X-rays, which revealed that I had three fractures of the skull and a broken nose. I was moved to the intensive care ward and, following further examination, the doctor confirmed I had a perforated eardrum (which resulted in my coping with life-long partial deafness), and a vision problem with my left eye. I was also suffering a mild coma.

At the time of my accident, my father had been working at our family doctor's house whitewashing the cellar walls; but when he received news of my accident, he quickly joined my mother at the hospital. The attending doctor described to my parents the complications that might arise as a result of my injuries. He said the next twenty-four hours would be very critical. He did not hold out much hope for my recovery, and he told them, "If your son sees the morning, he will be a lucky boy."

My parent took turns throughout that night keeping watch by my bedside while the nurses constantly monitored my condition. My mother and father were not regular churchgoers, but they spent a lot of time praying and blaming themselves for what had happened. Their worry and concern for my safe recovery continued through Sunday into Monday morning when the doctor, who had cared for me at the time of my admittance into the hospital, returned to the hospital and asked about the condition of the little boy who had been injured on Saturday. He was amazed, but very pleased, to find out I was still alive even though I was on the critical list. After evaluating my condition, he was able to tell my parents that there were now good signs for a slow, but certain recovery.

I spent many weeks in hospital recovering my health. The specialist thought that an operation might be necessary to correct the sight in my left eye. They reasoned that, in following the fall of the railings, my left eye turned toward my nose resulting in double vision. Every few days the eye specialist would check my vision and ask, "How many fingers can you see?" After about a month, my left eye slowly corrected itself. I no longer had double vision.

During my time in hospital, my parents visited me almost every day, especially my mother, who would often come straight to the hospital from the mill where she worked. I had missed so much school, but Miss Leah, my favourite teacher, visited me often bringing the material that I would need to know in preparation for the 13+ examinations to be held in late April. I was finally discharged from hospital and allowed to return home just before Christmas. Shortly before my thirteenth birthday in March, the doctors finally agreed that I was well enough to attend classes for full-time schooling. However, they said that I should not exert myself physically and to rest as much as possible. I still needed ongoing treatments, so that each week the ambulance would arrive to take me, along with my mother, to see the doctors and specialists.

It had been almost eight months since I last attended school. Because of Miss Leah's help and tutoring, I was able to quickly settle into a regular routine. I wrote my 13+ examination in late April and it was some weeks later that I got a letter that confirmed I had successfully, passed, thus allowing me to attend Stockport Technical School for Boys at Pendelbury Hall beginning in September 1947.

Because of all the extra effort, love and support I received from my parents and a dedicated teacher, I was given a chance to pursue a new direction in life studying for a vocation, despite having been brought up to expect a working-class future.

Some fifty-five years into the future, I was reunited with one of my classmates from Stockport Secondary Technical School for Boys. Peter Yarwood and I had both been students taking the same subject classes in the engineering course. We also shared our playtime together. Peter's parents were the landlords of the Black Horse Pub where, each Friday night, my father would spend the majority of his wages. The pub was a two-minute walk from our house in Ashton Court.

During our reunion discussions, the subject of the 13+ examinations came up. To his credit, Peter had excellent recall of those days back in 1947 and he offered the following humourous description:

"I vividly remember that examination and even some of the questions that were asked... mainly the maths questions. Strange, the old memory isn't it? If you were a resident in Cheshire and of a certain age one could take the entrance examination. I recall that there were over 400 candidates crammed into the main ballroom at Stockport Town Hall on Wellington Road North. Out of these, 48 were chosen to be 24 Engineering students and 24 Building students. We were destined to be educated to be foisted on to an unsuspecting world and to re-shape the post-war edifice of Great Britain and its far-flung Dominions.

I can remember the standing I obtained among the 48 fortunates, but I don't think I should embarrass you with that information. Anyway, I spent the next eight months or so keeping you under careful observation...

on account of the crack you'd had on your head...but slowly came to the conclusion that you were balmy before the accident"

It was a pity I never saw that Carnival because my sister, Audrey, was one of the participants as she marched in the parade along with her dance school members.

Chapter 2

THE BUGLE CALL — PART ONE

CLEANING OUT MY GARAGE every spring consists mainly of rearranging boxes, tools and decorating supplies accumulated over the past year. Although I know what most of the unopened boxes contain, occasionally I will open a box to remind myself of what is stored in there.

What memories I recalled when I opened such a box! There was the Boy Scouts' neckerchief that I wore in the late 1970's at the World Jamboree held in P. E. I., an old HO scale locomotive, a Christmas present bought for my son Paul, in 1972, the antique drafting set I received in 1954 and my tarnished and dimpled B-flat bugle from 1949. As I handled the old bugle, my mind went back to the time I spent as a bugle boy with the Stockport Sea Cadet Corps.

I was thirteen years old and attending the Stockport Technical School for Boys. I read a notice posted on the school bulletin board asking for boys, interested in joining the Sea Cadet Corps, to attend an information night at the Corps H.Q. Mr. Bertenshaw, the school janitor, was the C.O. of the local Sea Cadet Corps; he always hoped to attract new students into joining the cadet corps by posting this yearly notice.

I attended the information parade night along with several other fellow students. We were addressed by the Training Officer, Lt. Hadfield, who pointed out that, following a short period of recruit training, the cadets would then be given specialized cadet-training programmes. We visited various classes that included learning about the following: seamanship, semaphore, knots and splices, drill and marching. I was particularly interested in trying out as a drummer or a bugler in the band. The ship's company was given a stand-easy break during the evening at which time we visited the canteen to purchase cocoa and biscuits. It was interesting to see that, although the Sea Cadets were an all-boys' organization, two teenage girls were serving in the canteen! Before dismissal, the Commanding Officer noted that joining Sea Cadets could play a role in helping young recruits to become responsible adults in leadership roles. I did not hesitate to join.

For several weeks, we recruits paraded in civilian dress before we were given a pair of black, oily-looking boots and shown how to "spit and polish" them to get a high shine. Each parade night, our boots were inspected to check the quality of the shine. We engaged in basic drill and marching for the first half of the evening before we were dismissed for stand-easy. Following the break, we were instructed in seamanship, which consisted of naval terminology and history.

Finally, the night arrived when we were to be supplied with our uniforms. Each recruit was issued a uniform top and bell-bottoms and was told by the Supply Officer to, "Get your mother to do the alterations." A white cap with Tally band, a collar, and a black silk and white front were for summer wear; winter wear included a black cap, blue jersey and overcoat to be issued later in the training year. Recruits were instructed on the correct way of pressing the bell-bottoms, folding the black silk, ironing the collar and tying the Tally band bow at the side of the cap.

As the end of the training year approached, cadets were asked to sign up for summer camp to be held in Morecombe. Before joining cadets, I had never been away for more than a day's outing, going either to the seaside or to the Bellevue Zoo; so the chance to go to summer camp for two weeks was exciting. After enrolling, I was selected to join the advance party. The day before the ship's company was due to leave for the summer camp, we loaded all the camping equipment and supplies onto a large flatbed lorry. We cadets sat in the flatbed of the truck, but safe from danger because of the raised sides and tailboard. It rained heavily during the trip so that we crawled under a large, black tarpaulin to keep dry while the officers and senior NCOs travelled in the cab of the lorry or by car. We arrived at the camp, and after crawling out from under the canvas, we found ourselves covered in a black, oily film. However, we were ordered immediately to off-load the equipment and supplies. Several large tents for the cadet sleeping quarters and a marquee mess-tent were quickly set up next to the school, which was to be our headquarters. Only after we had completed all the work were we dismissed and able to use the school showers to wash off the black goo.

Most of the older cadets smoked, but never having smoked I often wondered what it would be like. My father always coughed and spluttered whenever he lit his "fag", especially first thing in the morning; I always wondered why he continued the habit! During one stand-easy break period, a cadet offered me a Grand Pasha — a Turkish, oval-shaped, flat cigarette. Like the other cadets, I gripped the cigarette between my finger and thumb breathing in as it was being lit. I coughed and wheezed and spluttered; my eyes watered and I felt nauseous. I wanted to stop, but another cadet urged me to keep breathing in and swallow the smoke. So I sucked in and swallowed, not once but twice. My head was spinning and I felt so dizzy that when I tried to stand up, I fell flat on my face. Everyone laughed, but it only made me more resolved to keep trying until I could smoke like all the other cadets, even blowing the smoke out of my nose! It would be many years before I finally quit.

Summer ended, we returned to school, and another cadet-training year began. I became interested in joining the band, as did John Bell, a fellow technical school student. He wanted to become a drummer while I was drawn to the bugle. I was given an old, tarnished bugle that I was to clean until it shone. Then I was told to practice blowing the bugle. "Spit in it," I was told, "to get a note!"

Most days after school and on weekends, I got out the silver polish and cleaned the brass and copper bugle till it shone — even the dented parts! Then I wrapped the bugle in a soft cloth to keep off fingerprints. To practice blowing the bugle, I had to stuff a sock down the bell-mouth to mute the noise, thus muffling the tone. Most times, I went down Tame Street and out into the local meadows where I could freely play as loudly as I wanted. Much as I tried, I had little success in spitting into the bugle to produce tones. I was beginning to feel that I would never succeed.

But I was determined to try a little harder. Finally, one day I produced my first bugle note; then a second followed, then a third and suddenly, I was playing the five-note scale. Since no one could read music all our bugle music was learned by ear and the tunes were played from memory. There were many pieces to learn and each had a distinctive name such as Long Tom, Hawkins, Semper Fidelis, Georgia. On a parade, the drum major would call out the name of the tune to be played and following drum rolls from the drum section, the bugle section played the tune.

Once a month, the bugle band would be out on parade leading a

Sunday school walk or participating in a local carnival parade. In my first major parade, we marched down the centre of Manchester, past City Hall, past huge crowds lining the pavement and cheering us on, and the drum and bugle music resounding off the walls of the buildings. I was still learning to play the bugle and, even though I went through all the motions, there was little sound coming from my bugle! We often travelled by coach to other towns in the Northwest of England to participate in parades. Sometimes, we were one of several bands in a parade; sometimes, we were the only band. Soon the excellent quality of our bugle band performance became well-known across the North of England.

The band comprised a drum major, four side drummers, a bass drummer, cymbal player and twelve buglers. When I became more adept at playing the bugle, I was selected as a solo bugler. My friend, John, had earned the position as solo drummer and led the drum section. A new cadet by the name of Alban Muldoon, who had originally tried out as a bugler, joined the drum section and quickly showed exceptional talent. I was not to know then that he would become my future brother-in-law!

We progressed through the cadet-training years and both John and I became proficient in all subjects. We were each promoted through the ranks to that of Petty Officer. We often found ourselves instructing the cadets in drill, or teaching classes in knots, or seamanship, or semaphore. As Petty Officers, we carried a lot of authority and we were expected to ensure that the cadets kept up to the standards laid down.

For most cadets, there was no need to remind them that short hair was a must, especially for band members. One weekend, just before a band parade, the bandmaster asked me to cut the hair of one of the buglers. Cadet George Kick's hair had grown over his ears, and since there was no time to give him a full haircut I decided to trim his hair straight over and above the ears. Unfortunately, along with the hair, I cut a thin slice off the top off his ear. After that, George always kept his hair cut short. The bandmaster would often threaten the cadets by saying, "Petty Officer Goostrey will cut your hair, if it's too long."

No one ever again forgot to get a haircut before going on parade.

THE BUGLE CALL — PART TWO

THROUGHOUT THE YEAR, BUGLE and trumpet band contests were held across the north of England. Band sections competed for trophies — bugles against bugle, trumpet against trumpet, and all bands competed on an equal basis for trophies awarded for deportment, drum major and drum section.

Each band's successes were compiled, with the winner receiving the Best Band of the day award. Boys Brigade, Army Cadets, St. John's Ambulance Brigade, Scout Troops and Sea Cadets represented bugle bands. The Air Training Cadets and Girls Training Corps and Scout Troops represented trumpet bands. Under the direction of our bandmaster, Chief Petty Office George Bury, our band reached the peak of its perfection during the early 1950's. The Stockport Sea Cadets Bugle Band set the standard against which all other bugle bands in the north of England were judged

On occasions, the band travelled alone — no parents or girl friends — and then we would often break into our bawdy versions of songs such as; 'Twas on the Good Ship Venus, She's a Big Girl, Fat Girl. We would each bring our butties (sandwiches) to eat on the bus but I was never sure what mine would be made with. John's butties were always made with Marmite, which he didn't like, but I loved! John's mother had a soft spot for me; she always said I was like another son to her, and she told John he could share his butties with me.

One day, we faced competition with the Coventry School of Music band. This band had never before entered competitions in the north of

England. We were told that it was a trumpet band so that they would not be our competitors and, unless they could march or drum better than we could, we had no concern. The bugle contests were always held first. Each band in turn marched and countermarched into position and played its test piece. Then the solo bugler marched to the front to play his chosen piece. During performances, the judges would be evaluating deportment, the drumming, the drum major and the solo and a band test piece. The trumpet band contest followed the bugle band contest. This new band, the Coventry School of Music trumpet band, had been drawn to play in last position.

It was the finest band I have ever heard. They wore uniforms of white hats, red tunics and blue trousers. You might have thought that they were the Royal Marine Band, rather than a cadet band. The band included the drum major, six side drummers, a bass drummer, two tenor drummers and complemented by eighteen trumpeters. Their deportment was superb, and we had never before heard trumpets played to such a high calibre. On that day, they picked up every trophy for which they were eligible, while we were only able to win the bugle test piece and my bugle solo trophies. Meeting up with this band made us realize that, in the future, we could not expect to just turn up. Fortunately, the Coventry band did not attend all the same competitions as we did, because they were located in the Midlands, where they spent most of their contest time.

In the early 1950's, our greatest rivalry developed in competing against the Brighouse St. John's Ambulance Brigade. The first time we played against them, we felt rather smug because, in the past, we had never seen a St. John's Ambulance Brigade that could march well, let alone play a good bugle test piece. Although Brighouse in Yorkshire was famous for its Colliery Brass Band, which was one of the best in the country, we couldn't expect a bugle band of any calibre from a St. John's Ambulance Brigade. But they always came to win, and each time we competed we soon realized they were as good as we were in each of the areas of competition. For a number of years, we would alternate first place finishes and share the bugle trophies between us. Although competition was intense, many friendships that would last for many years, developed between individual members of bands. In 2003, as a measure of this friendship, my brother-in-law Alban, a past member of the 1950's Sea Cadet band was the Guest of Honour at the 50th Anniversary celebration of the Brighouse St. John's Ambulance Brigade.

At the age of nineteen, I gave up my role as a solo bugler because I was promoted to Drum Major. After several years in the ranks of the band, I was now leading the band on a parade, calling out the bugle tunes, and responsible for the dress and deportment of both the band and myself. The authority and control shown by the drum major over his band were recognized at band contests, and I was successful in winning a number of awards.

Prior to my role as drum major, I had won many solo bugle contests during my years as a bugler. In 1950, I competed in the local Stockport Band Contest. All the competing bands had completed their performances and were formed up for the awards ceremony. As each prize was announced, the winner would march out to receive his trophy. "The winner of the bugle solo prize is awarded to Stockport Sea Cadets", came the announcement. I was really excited and proud as I smartly marched out to receive the trophy — a silver bugle. After saluting the presenter, I turned and started back to my position with my band. Then an announcement came, saying that a mistake had been made and the solo bugle prize should have been awarded to another band. I was confused and upset but more embarrassed to have to return the trophy in front of all my friends, family and the townspeople. Although I had to return the trophy, I proved that I could hold my head up even in defeat as I marched back to the front, saluted smartly and handed back the award before returning to my position. Many people in attendance felt that it was wrong to ask for the trophy's return and that a second bugle trophy should have been made available for the winner.

In the late 1950's, after I had been promoted to Chief Petty Officer, I stepped down as Drum Major to become Bandmaster. But the years had taken their toll on the Stockport Sea Cadet Bugle Band. Many of the members, with whom I had spent the last ten years, retired from the Corps – some to serve their National Service, some to get married and some had simply left. With time, the calibre of the band changed and the quality was no longer there. We went to fewer band contests because we were really no longer good enough to compete. The band members became demoralized as we rarely succeeded winning awards in the competitions.

Many of my fellow cadets had left the corps to join the army, air force or navy. It was a time when National Service was in force and all young men were expected to serve two years in the military, once they had reached their eighteenth birthday. Deferment was allowed until you were twenty-one, if requested by the company for whom you worked.

My best friend, John, had joined the navy and I also hoped to do the same when I was twenty-one. However, when that time came, I was turned down for National Service because I had a perforated ear drum, the result of the accident I sustained at the age of twelve. After all those years, I knew that it was time to leave Sea Cadets and in 1958 I retired. During the twelve years that I was in the band as a bugler, a drum major and a bandmaster, I had grown from being a boy into being a man.

My band experience as a leader and teacher developed in me a sense of responsibility and confidence that would enable me to pursue whatever career I chose to follow in my future life.

Chapter 3

BORN IN THE DEPRESSION

Today, as I look out over my garden from my kitchen window, watching the birds fighting over the peanuts laid out for them in the old iron pot, and seeing the humming birds flit here and there between the flowers and the bird feeder, my mind often wanders back to my past life, so different from the idyllic life I now lead.

How could I have possibly guessed that as a young kid who wore old clothes, who sometimes wore clogs, who wiped his nose on his sleeve and who often forgot to wash behind his ears or to clean his teeth could end up living here in the Village of Wellington located in beautiful Prince Edward County on the edge of Lake Ontario? Why I made certain decisions that have changed both my lifestyle and my profession and allowed me to spend more than half my life in a new country, take much reflection. When I came to understand the working-class socioeconomic lifestyle into which I was born, I quickly learned my place in life, even though I may not have understood why. The English class system has long divided the royals from the gentry and the gentry from the workers so that you soon came to know your place within the system. One had to be careful not to step over the line. It all depended upon which side of the track you came from, or whether you were from "upstairs or downstairs."

I was a love child, born on March 25, 1934, into a working-class family in the industrial town of Stockport in the Northwest of England. My father, Harry, was tall and good-looking with black, curly hair. He was in good physical condition. He was not interested in school and spent most of his days working some menial jobs and playing sports the rest of the time. May, my mother, was a conscientious student, who worked hard at her studies. She earned a scholarship, which would have given her the opportunity to attend high school. However, my grandparents had little money and certainly none to spend on higher education, so my mother gave up her schooling to work a forty-eight hours a week in the mill. During her teen years, she became a member of the local Salvation Army serving as a Sunshine Girl.

How Harry and May ever got together I cannot say, but they fell madly in love and wanted to get married. She was six years younger than Harry and since she was not yet twenty-one her parents would not give their permission. Grandma Mellor, especially, saw Harry as a wastrel and a good-for-nothing. Harry and May sought advice on how they could get married without permission. They would have to create a reason for marriage before May turned twenty-one. They were married in October 1933. I was born six months later.

I was born in a small, one-up and one-down terraced house my parents rented. Although my mother worked hard to make the house a home, they found it too small and before long they moved to a larger house, two-up and two-down, in Ashton Court. The location was much more convenient since it was closer to the mill where my mother worked. She often told me over the years what a good baby I was in those early years. She would tell me, "I only needed to feed you, change you and put you in your pram and you would sleep until your next feed." At this time, Harry worked for a local brewery where he learned to drive a lorry so that he could deliver kegs of beer to pubs within the town. This job might well be the reason why, on his way home from work, he spent much of his time in the local pubs on Great Portwood Street. There were several pubs along the main street, but his favourite was the Black Horse.

As I was growing up, I became aware of my father's expressed jealousy toward anyone who was educated, even my mother. I now believe that he felt inadequate because of his failure to get a better education when he was younger. I always wondered how my father and mother could be so attached to each other, especially since my father often argued with her. Most arguments would end with comments such as, "You bloody people with an education . . ." Perhaps, had he applied himself to learning and achieving higher education, the tense family atmosphere in which I grew up would not have existed.

My earliest memory of those times was the day my sister was born.

I was almost four years old, and I remember having to wait outside our house in the courtyard with my father while the midwife delivered the baby. "Harry, you have a beautiful little girl," she called out as she leaned from the upstairs window announcing the arrival of the new baby. The midwife and my father and mother discussed what to name the baby since the birth had to be registered that day. Having agreed on the baby's name, my father went off to record her birth while I was left in the care of my Granny Goostrey, who lived near by. When asked by the registrar for the baby's name, Harry said, "Yvonne." However, he was unable to spell the name correctly, so he changed it to Audrey, which he could spell. My sister has related this story to me more than once since then. How surprised she was when, many years later, I married a lady named Yvonne!

To say we were a loving family is difficult for me to admit. Although we were cared for, kept clean and tidy and had enough to eat, I cannot remember my father ever saying he loved us and in return I can never remember saying we loved him. He may well have been proud of some of the things we achieved as we grew, but he rarely showed it. I think that any time we achieved successes in our schooling it must have been like a thorn in his side.

We lived in Ashton Court. The name might suggest an affluent residence but it was really a hole in the wall. The houses were built around a courtyard with several shops located on the main street side of Great Portwood Street. Many houses stood on two of the remaining sides, and across the backside of the block, lived a carpenter whose main business was building coffins. Some of the houses were split back-to back, so anyone living in these houses had only the one door to enter and leave. My grandparents lived on Tame Street, and their house was built back-to back with our house. Had we knocked a doorway in the common wall we could have lived together!

A brick outbuilding, which spanned the width of the court, contained the loos (lavatories), with three families sharing one. Dustbins for each family were placed against the wall. Often, the door to our loo was closed and more than once, when it was occupied at night, I would pee against the dustbin wall. When the blocks of houses were originally built, some had been reserved for the upper working-class management, and unlike the back-to-back houses for the working class, these houses not only had their own front and rear door, but also had their own private outdoor loo and back yard.

It was a common sight, each weekend, to see the housewives cleaning their flagstone doorsteps and windowsills with a donkey stone dipped in water. The sandstone block added a wet layer of coloured paste to the stones, which upon drying left a rich brown or cream-coloured patina on the front step and windowsills. The housewives also shared with their husbands the task of whitewashing the walls of their houses as well as the loo.

Much of our local shopping was done on Great Portwood Street. Among those shops included a butcher's, a hardware store, a grocery, a haberdashery, a newsagent, a fish shop, as well as the local pubs and the Chippy. Each of the shops had a small yard with a private loo. A wooden door, usually bolted, blocked the yard off from the court. The shopkeepers' only complaint was with children playing ball games, and then trying to sneak over the gate to retrieve a ball that had landed in one of their yards.

Foster's fish shop was behind the centre gate along the court wall and early, each morning, the fish truck would arrive and park on Tame Street close to the entry, which allowed access into the Court. Harold, the driver, would off-load the barrels of fish packed in ice, then roll them down the entry into the Court and into the shop yard. There was always a pungent smell of fish in the air and in the summer time lots of flies — big, juicy bluebottles — flew around your head. Harold was slightly built but immensely strong from the years of lifting and moving the great, heavy wooden barrels. You never gave him any lip because, if you did, he would pick you up as if you were a feather, turn you upside down and shove your head and shoulders into an empty, smelly fish barrel until you cried out to be free. He would not let go until you said you were sorry. But he was also generous, often giving the children a fish to take home. " Give that to your Mam," he would say as he rolled the barrel past the house.

The local area was not totally devoid of open space even though we seemed to be surrounded by houses, shops, mills, gasworks and railway sidings. A local chapel, which was surrounded by low stonewalls, was located on the opposite side of Tame Street. The walls were not too high and we could easily climb on top and practice our "tightrope walking." At times, we would draw three straight lines up the wall with chalk to represent wickets, and then play cricket in the street. More than once, someone hit a tennis ball or kicked a soccer ball through a window and we would quickly run away hoping not to get caught. Past the blocks of houses and along the high, brick wall, which separated the railway shunting yards from Tame Street, we could quickly escape the poverty, dirt and grime of our surroundings. A few minutes walk would bring us to open fields, trees and to the River Tame, where we would fish and swim in the summer time.

Life was good to us with our families and friends close by, but we were not to know that a war was about to bring major changes to our lives.

Chapter 4

MY EARLY EDUCATION

GETTING AN EDUCATION HAS always been important to me. As I matured, I could see that I would need a solid educational foundation on which to build for the future; on looking back on my Primary school years in the days when I lived in my hometown of Stockport, I realize I was not a good student.

I attended Portwood School at the age of five. I was very fortunate in that the school was located across the main street from our house. The school was Edwardian in design — a two- storey stone building erected during the Industrial Revolution. I do not know what it was used for when first built, but it was a very impressive building. However, by 1939, the smoke and the grime had changed the stone walls from varying shades of grey to black. A playground, with ornate, iron railings on top of the low wall, was located in front of the school. This barrier prevented children from running out onto the street where the cars and tramcars ran up and down Great Portwood Street. In those early days, my mother would take me to school even though it was only across the street from where I lived. I cannot remember what specific lessons we were taught, but I enjoyed a lot of playtime. The three R's were certainly instilled in those early days because I can remember having to learn how to spell and read, as well as singing as part of the programme. I spent hours holding a steel-nib pen, dipped into an inkwell, to practise ABC's and 123's on lined paper after having been instructed to keep the capital letters, small letters and numbers in straight lines. While I remember the names of two of the teachers from that time, Miss Margeson and

Miss Dixon, I cannot remember what subjects they taught. Perhaps one of them was the music teacher?

I attended Portwood School for four years before moving to Vernon Park Primary School. Students attended this school until they were either eleven or thirteen years old and their leaving was dependant upon their passing the 11+ or 13+ exams. When I attended Vernon Park School, I had to walk about a mile by going across Great Portwood Street, down Queen Street and across the River Goyt Bridge to Alpine Road where the school was situated halfway up the road. Alpine Road was well-named because it was actually a hill, which got gradually steeper as you climbed until, for support, you had to hang on to a railing, which ran up the centre of the road. From the top of Alpine Road you could look down over the whole school and across toward Great Portwood Street from where you could almost see where I lived.

The school was larger than Portwood School but it was also surrounded by a low stone wall surmounted with tall, iron railings. There were two entrance gates to the school playground area located on the side. The building was constructed of glazed brick, which reflected the sunshine whenever it could penetrate the smoky haze from the nearby gas works.

Vernon Park School classrooms were on one level unlike Portwood School where we had stairs to climb. The classrooms were arranged around a central open area where, each day, all the children and the teachers gathered to hold the opening exercises. It was customary to sing, "God Save the King" and recite "The Lord's Prayer", after which, the head master would address the assembly. At the end of opening exercises, we would be duly marched out class by class to start the day's routine.

The headmaster at Vernon Park School, Mr. Kitchen, was a stern-looking man, who wore a grey, pinstriped suit. His hair was sleeked down, flat. Over his black-rimmed glasses, he would peer down at you, his hands held behind his back, partly hiding the cane he often carried — an instrument of punishment — which I think he took great delight in using. There were always students waiting at his office for the inevitable, "Hold out your hand, boy", when he returned from a tour around the school or a visit with one of the staff. On more than one occasion, I was one of those boys. I have very little memory of what schoolwork I did, but I know that we had a music programme and I became proficient in singing. We were never taught how to read music, all the singing being learned by ear. We practised the anthem of every country in the

British Commonwealth, to be sung by the classes whenever there was an appropriate occasion.

I had an acceptable singing voice, and my teachers recommended that I audition for the Stockport Boys' Choir, which was run by a Dr. Dauber. I received approval to attend an audition, and having passed, I became a member of the boys' choir. For some months, I attended choir practice; as we spent hour after hour practising scales, I soon found that I was becoming bored so I stopped going. When I was a member, I was asked many times by my Grandma Goostrey to sing her favourite hymn. I used to stand by the side of her chair and sing, "There Is a Green Hill Far Away." She always said how much she loved that old hymn and, many times after singing for her, she would give me a threepenny bit to buy some toffee. I don't know whether I sang for her enjoyment or for the toffee!

My favourite teacher was Mrs. Leah — a wonderful, caring teacher, who taught arithmetic. She was to play an important role in my life at the time of my 13+ examinations. I had thrown away my chance of going to Grammar School having failed my 11+ examinations. Maybe, subconsciously, I had not wanted to pass because I believed that going to Grammar School was reserved for those who were wealthy, or for those whose fathers went to work in suits and ties, or for those whose mothers did not work in the mill. That was my perception of the educational class structure. However, I began to make an effort toward learning the information that I would need to pass the 13+ examinations to be written in a year and a half.

It was less than a year after the 11+ examinations that I suffered serious injuries in an accident from which I was not expected to recover.

Chapter 5

CLARENCE ON THE MENU

THE HOUSE IN WHICH I presently live is located in a beautiful rural area, surrounded by open fields and trees. It is centrally heated in winter and air conditioned in summer. The house is not large, but there is still more available space than is needed for two people. It is quite different from the house in which I grew up — Number 2 Ashton Court!

There were three levels to the house: a coal cellar, a main floor, and a second floor. It was a small house in terms of liveable square footage, probably not more than 350 square feet in total. The kitchen, positioned on the left as you entered the house, was around 5 feet by 8 feet. A window measuring 3 feet by 4 feet was located on one of the longer walls. A shallow fieldstone sink was positioned below the window. A tiny workspace counter was placed to the left of the sink and to the right, a gas stove for cooking. The window could not be opened; it had been painted shut, and although it faced a blank wall, some light found its way in. However, on the wall over the counter space was a gaslight, the only means of illuminating the kitchen when it got dark. The house door took up the rest of the wall space. A cupboard along the other long wall was used for storing foodstuff and kitchen supplies. A zinc bathtub hung on the wall, below which was a galvanized washtub. Across the corner of the kitchen, stood a built-in steel tub for boiling water for laundry and below that was a small fireplace to heat the water.

The living room, an area 10 feet x 12 feet, was located to the right of the door. On the left was an alcove, containing an upright gramophone player and a small cupboard. A wide chimneybreast, housing a built-in cast-iron fireplace with an oven, projected into the room a short distance. A floor-to-ceiling cupboard on the other side of the fireplace was divided into two portions, the upper being longer than the lower.

Thinking of this cupboard, reminds me of a time when my father, whose work took him away from home for weeks, returned late in October, with a live chicken under his coat. Of course, we were very excited and wondered what we would do with a chicken. It did not take him long to remove the lower doors of the cupboard and replace them with a wire-mesh barrier. After spreading some straw on the cupboard floor, he fenced in the chicken. We named the chicken Clarence, who became our family pet! My sister and I cared for him and cleaned out his coop. More than once Clarence escaped our grip when we let him out of the coop. He flew around the house, and sometimes, he settled long enough on a chair for us to capture him and return him to the cupboard. Once, Clarence flew too close to the gaslight fixture taking off the mantle just like my father, who being tall, invariably knocked off the mantle with his head! On Christmas Eve, my sister and I went shopping with my mother, and when we returned, we could not find Clarence. His coop was deserted. He had gone! My father had wrung his neck, plucked the feathers, cleaned and stuffed the carcass ready for Christmas dinner. Clarence, nicely roasted, lay on the table that Christmas Day but no one, except my father, ate the chicken.

Clarence was not our only pet.

In early 1940, my father, who had enlisted in the Royal Artillery, was home on leave for a short time before being shipped off to the Far East. My mother had allowed my sister and me to have a pet, a small mongrel puppy that slept at the side of the bed during the night. It was a time when, on a nightly basis, the Germans were bombing railways, factories and dockyard areas.

Not far north of where we lived were located the Manchester Ship Canal and dockyards. Most nights, we could clearly see the glow of the fires, which were started by the incendiary bombs dropped on the dockyard area. Unless the sirens went off, we were at liberty to stay in our homes. One night, while my father was still on leave, a German bomber on its way back from its mission to bomb the dockyards, jettisoned a remaining bomb over our area, which exploded about a mile from where we lived. Everyone jumped up at the sound. In his haste, my father accidentally stepped on the puppy, which reacted by biting my father on his toe. He shot into the air landing on the bed, full weight. The corner of the bed collapsed, causing my mother to roll off onto the floor. We grabbed our nightclothes, because the sirens were sounding and we had to go to the air-raid shelters. A few hours later, the all clear sounded, and we returned home. We entered the house and my father lit the gas mantle. When the room filled with light, we looked up to see the leg of the bed sticking down through the ceiling! Before he returned to his barracks, he was able to repair the ceiling for my mother.

In the corner, opposite the large cupboard which had once been home to Clarence, was a door which led down to the coal cellar — a dark, dank and dirty place, down which you needed to take a lighted candle in order to retrieve a bucket of coal. There was no other light down there, except for the small chink of light, which came from the grid that covered the coal chute. As well as the door to the cellar, this living-room wall contained another door, leading to the upstairs. A large window on the remaining wall provided sufficient natural light during the day. I cannot remember ever seeing this window open.

At the side of this window was a small shelf mounted on the wall, on which sat a radio, powered by a wet-cell battery. Below the shelf, stood an oak chair. Whenever I sat in this chair, I had to make sure that my head did not strike the edge of the shelf. One night, in my late teens, I had been out drinking with the boys, something I rarely ever did. Coming into the house, I could see my mother looking at me queerly. I sat down on the old oak chair and whacked my skull across the ledge of the shelf. Under normal circumstances, this blow would have knocked me out. My mother stared at me and shouted, "Roy! You're drunk!" With a glazed expression and giggling, I replied, "Who me?" That was the only time I ever came home in that state.

A gaslight fixture hung down from the centre of the ceiling so that the gas mantle was six feet above the floor. Pulling on a chain, which opened the gas valve, controlled the flow of gas. Pulling an opposite chain would allow you to turn the gas off. The dining table was always placed under the gas lamp because the mantle was not protected by a glass shade. On many occasions, when the table was moved away from under the mantle, my father would forget and often walk below it, taking off the filament with his head! Mounted on the ceiling of the living room but closer to the fireplace, was a clothes rack. This rack could be raised and lowered by means of a rope over a pulley, and was a convenient way of drying clothes whenever it rained, which was on most laundry days.

The stairs were quite steep leading up to the bedrooms where we all slept. My mother and father slept in the larger room together with my sister, who slept in her own bed. The room had a large window, which was the same size as the downstairs living-room window. There was a small fireplace in this bedroom built directly above the downstairs fireplace, and on rare occasions, when it got really cold, my parents would light the fire. Most times, however, early in the evening, we would place two bricks in the oven at the side of the living-room fireplace, and then at bedtime, my mother would wrap each brick in a towel — one for me, one for my sister — so we each had a hot brick to warm the ice-cold sheets.

Attached to the main bedroom and located directly above the kitchen was a small box room with a sloping ceiling. This was my bedroom. It contained a small window, like the kitchen window, but this one could be opened to let in fresh air. The bedrooms contained a small chest of drawers for personal clothing or extra bedding. The rooms each had a wall-mounted gaslight, but they were not used, because we always lit candles when we went to bed.

Because there was no loo in the house, we used a chamber pot, which in our case was a white-enamelled bucket. Each morning, my mother emptied and cleaned the pot for the next use. On occasions, my mother would ask me to empty the bucket; I was always embarrassed to walk through the Court to the loos knowing that everyone knew what I was doing. I don't really know why I was embarrassed, because everyone else was doing the same thing.

My parents moved to this house when I was still a baby. I grew up there, went to school from there, went to work from there, did my courting from there and finally got married from there. In total, I lived there for twenty-five years and, in retrospect, never really yearned to live anywhere else, even though it would have been beneficial to have our own indoor plumbing and electric lighting. Number 2 Ashton Court no longer exists. It was demolished, along with much of the surrounding area, to be replaced by the M 63, a modern high-speed extension of the motorway system, which runs throughout England today. It runs along the area that was once the old railway line.

There are still glimpses of parts of the neighbourhood, but mostly, it exists only in the memories of those who lived there.

Chapter 6

APPRENTICESHIP YEARS

I HAVE ALWAYS BEEN GOOD at drawing, even as a youngster. I often spent time sketching cartoon characters, airplanes and faces of film stars and pop artists. When my children were young, I painted their bedroom walls with their favourite popular images. When I attended technical school, my interest in drawing helped me to develop proficiency in engineering drawing, and I dreamed that, one day, I could become an engineering draftsman or designer. However, everyone I knew worked with their hands, either in the mills or on the shop floor in a factory. I believed that there was no other future for me.

In April 1949, I ended my formal schooling at Stockport Technical School for Boys having completed the two-year engineering course. I could have applied to attend Stockport College, our local college, to undertake an additional year of education and technical skill training, but I was eager to obtain an apprenticeship and begin earning money. Wasting time taking more educational courses seemed foolish at the time. Another wage packet coming into the household was more beneficial to my mother. Besides, my father had never pushed me to, "Get an education, lad!"

At the time I left Stockport Technical School, both my father and my uncle Bill, were working for a local engineering company called Bolton's Super-Heater and Pipe Works. Uncle Bill, who was older than my father, had worked at this company for many years and was close to retirement. He worked as a blacksmith's striker — the man who pounds the sledgehammer to assist the blacksmith as he shapes the forging.

You needed to be very strong to do this type of work. He always loved telling me his favourite story taken from his military service in the Boer war. Once, when out on patrol, he became detached from his company during a violent sandstorm. He was lost in the desert, wandering for several days before being rescued by his company. He said he survived by drinking camel urine and chewing on its dung. Whether the story was true or not, I will never know.

My father said that Bolton's Super-Heater was looking for a school-leaver who was interested in getting an apprenticeship as a tool and die maker — a highly skilled trade in the engineering field. Eagerly, I attended an interview with the tool-room foreman. He asked many questions in testing my knowledge. Could I read a blueprint? Did I know how to read a micrometer? Was I able to sharpen my own cutting tools? Following the interview, I was given a tour of each of the workstations in the tool room and then introduced to the tradesmen. If I were to be chosen for an apprenticeship with the company, I would be working under the direction and guidance of Bill Kemp, one of the senior tool and die makers.

I had never before received letters directed to me, but shortly after the visit to Bolton's, a letter arrived offering me a position as a four-year apprentice tool and die maker. I would be given some day release to attend Stockport College; also, I would be expected to attend night school classes to supplement my previous education. I soon learned that the extra year I could have taken as a school-leaver would now become part of my apprenticeship. Now that I needed to attend night school, I hoped that the time would not conflict with my Sea Cadet parades and band practice.

On my first day at Bolton's, I was introduced to my apprenticeship supervisor, Bill Kemp. He was more than six feet tall, wearing clean, smartly pressed overalls. His black hair was slicked back, flat and smooth with a clean parting, as though it had been cut with a knife. I asked him how he kept his hair so neat and tidy and he explained that he used a liquid Silica Gel, which keeps hair in place until it is washed.

During the first few weeks on the job, I found myself mostly "running and fetching," rather than doing any practical work. If I wasn't bringing tea from the canteen for everyone in the tool room, I was running to the local tobacconists for packets of fags. I was always told, "And remember, don't let anyone see you."

Often, I had to go to the parts department to collect items for a jig, or a fixture that was under construction in the toolroom. It was in these early days of visiting that department where I almost became a victim of a sexual predator. "Fat Harry," the only name I ever knew him by, was the storekeeper responsible for all the parts located in that area. For security reasons, the department, which included a glassed-in office area, was screened off from the main shop floor area by high, sheet metal walls. A service counter and a wire-screen door led into the department. Shelving spaces were laid out in horizontal racks inside the walls, and in the far corners, well away from view, were stacked boxes and sacks of soft items such as paper and rags. It was a perfect place for a quick smoke, or even a snooze. You could not be seen unless you actually walked into the storage area. I had been told by my supervisor Bill, as well as other tradesmen in the tool room, to "Watch out for Harry," but I had no idea what they were talking about.

Harry was short, fat and balding, always pleasant to talk to and always ready to show you where to get the items you wanted from his department. However, each time I went into the store after showing me where the item was located, he encouraged me to reach up to get it while "accidentally" rubbing against me. Whenever I leaned over the sacks and boxes to collect items, Harry pressed himself against me. At first, I was not aware of his intentions, but one day he asked me to put my hand into his overalls and then I saw that his fly was open. I became frightened and unsure of what to do. After all, he was a company foreman; since I was taller and physically stronger than him, I threatened to beat him up if he didn't stop. He said that I did not understand, that he was only trying to reach over me to help. On my return to the toolroom, I told the senior foreman and Bill, my supervisor, what happened in the parts department. They were both very upset and Arthur, the tool-room foreman, left to confront Harry about the incident. The works manager was also told what had happened and within a few days, Harry was relocated to another area of plant.

My apprenticeship training continued, and soon I was developing the skills required to become a tool and die maker. While Bill directed most of my training in machining, shaping and tool grinding, other members of the toolroom guided my training. George showed me the way to surface-grind and shape; Russell gave me instructions on the lathe; and Harold, a really old gentleman, taught me all he knew about bench-work layout, filing and scraping. He was a very remarkable man, well past retirement, who was an expert in that he created most of his own precision measuring equipment. His micrometer, vernier and sine bars were second to none, and they were as accurate as any you could purchase. I got along with all the men in the toolroom but I soon came to dislike Russell, although I believe it was my fault for what happened.

I was asked to make a sample lathe part and, after removing the work that had been set up at the lathe, I started to machine the part I was to produce. A very hard, flat-handed slap across the side of my head sent me staggering across the shop. It was Russell, telling me that I must never remove another man's set-up without asking permission. He was right, but I had not been warned. Later, from my own experience, I found that it took considerable time to correctly set up a machine for some manufactured parts.

Although my apprenticeship training was centred in the toolroom, I was moved around to various other departments on the shop floor in order to appreciate how they all related to one another. I spent a few weeks working in the parts department, handing out and recording products that were used throughout the company.

Mark Brettel was the foreman of the Inspection Department where all items were quality-checked, receiving a stamp of approval before being passed on to the customer. I worked in that department with Mark for about four weeks. He knew that I was attending night school, and he was always interested in how well I was getting on with my subjects. In fact, I was failing, and I felt guilty in assuring Mark that I was doing well. I had stretched myself to the limit because of my involvement with the Sea Cadets, and more than once I missed classes in order to attend parade nights or band practice. Mark wanted me to obtain my A.M.I.Mech.E. (Associate Member of the Institute of Mechanical Engineers) which required a serious commitment to my evening school. I loved the drafting and mechanical technology classes, but I detested the mathematics classes. Even though only three subjects were required, I had to pass all of them; failing any of the subjects meant that the entire year had to be repeated. I failed my first year, with 49% in mathematics. There was no rewrite, so applying myself assiduously, I wrote those examinations for the second time and passed all subjects, receiving a mark of 100% in mechanical drafting. Few students had ever achieved such a high mark. The excellence of my drafting mark earned me a Whitworth Scholarship from the college. It had no monetary value, but it allowed me to select two engineering reference books for my future studies. After leaving the inspection department, I returned to the toolroom to continue my tool and die apprenticeship training.

As part of my training program, I wanted to spend time in the company's drawing office hoping, that with my ability in drawing, I would be able to fulfill my dream of becoming a design draftsman. With my mark in drafting and a Whitworth Scholarship, I felt that I finally would have that opportunity. At Bolton's Super-Heater and Pipe Works, it was not what you know, but whom you know. The social class structure was obvious even there. Because I had no connections at the management level, my request to be considered for time in the drawing office was turned down. As an apprentice, you were expected to be able to fully understand the drawings, but play no role in preparing them. I felt let down and decided to look for a new job. Because I now had two years' experience in a tool and die shop, and had attained good drafting skills at night school, I knew I had the qualifications for a job, should the opportunity arise.

In our local weekly newspaper, the *Stockport Express*, a small engineering company in the town had posted an employment advertisement requiring a junior draftsman. I had never applied for a job by letter before. Although I was uncertain as to what to say, I carefully outlined my workshop experience and drafting ability and sent the letter to the attention of the Technical Director, Mr. Eric Staniforth. This company's weird name — SISIS — was derived from the first letters of: Steel is Strength in Structure. It is interesting that the company was more often referred to as W. Hargreaves and Sons, the business having been founded by a gentleman called William Hargreaves. He had always been interested in turf culture — the maintenance and upkeep of quality grass surfaces by aeration, rolling, fertilizer spreaders, and such.

A few days later, I received a reply asking me to attend an interview at his home on the following Saturday morning. During the interview, Eric asked a lot of questions about my schooling and training. I was also asked to make simple sketches of items that allowed Eric to evaluate my drawing ability. He told me that much of my work would involve sketching, but while I thought I was good enough to do much more detailed drawing work, it would allow me a start in a drawing office. At the end of the interview, he offered me the job. I could start in two weeks. Bill Kemp was rather sorry to hear that I was leaving the apprenticeship at Bolton's, but he and everyone else in the tool room wished me well in my new job.

I started work with W. Hargreaves and Sons in September 1951. As the junior draftsman, most of the drawings that I did for Eric were small parts sketches, mainly on squared paper, complete with a carbon copy for records. Eric would give me a rough-sketched outline of an item, which I then set up in a more formal layout as a detailed drawing on tracing paper. One of my extra duties was to make the blueprints. I think their blue printer came out of the Ark! I had never seen such a blue printer, before or since. It consisted of a large, wooden frame fronted with glass, a felt pad the size of the glass and a hinged, wooden back. To make a print, the back was opened, in order to remove the felt pad, before placing the tracing-paper drawing face down on the glass. After cutting a piece of light sensitive blueprint paper, the same size as the tracing, the sensitive side was placed on the tracing. Then the felt pad was replaced and the hinged backing closed. The whole thing weighed a ton. You then needed to carry the frame outside to expose the glass to the light. As the light passed through the tracing, the blueprint paper turned white and the trick was to catch it before it turned too white. Then I had to rush inside, remove the exposed blueprint paper and place it in a large bath of cold water. Of course, it came out like a wet blanket and had to be hung up to dry. It reminded me of my mother, hanging out the laundry on washing day. Surprisingly, the white sheet turned blue, except where the drawn lines had restricted the light, and the lines stayed white. What an introduction into making a blueprint! I was to make many of them by this fashion until the day the company finally bought a blueprint machine.

Eric was adept at mechanical design. His skills in solving mechanical problems led to the design and production of equipment for use in horticulture. Through his guidance, I was to develop the ability to invent solutions for designs, which would become company products. But that was an era when there was still a need to trace formal drawings in ink, something that is rarely seen or used by draftsmen today. Computer-aided drawings and the ability of software to resolve drafting problems are the way designs are created today. Some junior engineers will never experience having to trace in ink, often spilling the ink all over the drawing and having to start over again. What a frustrating experience!

However, having had experience in freehand sketching, in pencilled detailed drawing, in preparing ink on velum tracings, in producing blueprints and whiteprints, as well as experiencing and using modern CAD options, helped to make me far more versatile in my chosen field.

Chapter 7

EVERYTHING ON TICK

A T THIS STAGE OF my life, I think it fair to say that I am content with everything that is integral in my day-to-day existence. I am proud of my children and grandchildren and their accomplishments. I am happily married to a wonderful lady. We own a comfortable house, drive a new car and I am financially secure. When I look back at my progress through life, I measure my success, in large part, by comparing how far I have come to the times when we " 'ad nowt."

Growing up as a young boy in Stockport, there was little money coming into the house to pay for rent, food, or clothing. In the early days of the war, the hand-me-down clothes that my sister and I wore were either too big or too small, but always clean. The darned holes in my socks often got re-darned, and my vest sometimes stuck out of the worn patch in the seat of my short pants. When the soles of my shoes wore down so much that I could stick my finger through the holes, I inserted pieces of cardboard to cover them. That didn't prevent my feet from getting wet or from freezing numb in very cold weather, and sticking them close to the fire often resulted in getting chilblains. Because my toes swelled and itched so much from scratching and rubbing them raw, I often cried myself to sleep. It was so painful that I could not put my shoes on without crushing the swellings.

While I was attending technical school, it was mandatory to wear the school uniform: gray slacks, a white shirt and school tie, a black blazer with the school crest, and black shoes. I was proud of my uniform and thought I looked a right "toff" when I was dressed for school. I took great care of my school uniform, always changing into my play clothes when I returned home.

When I joined sea cadets, I was shown how to clean, press and iron my uniform. I applied the same techniques to my personal clothing. I was always keen to produce the best possible spit-and-polish shine on my parade boots by polishing the toecaps and heels to gleam like black marble. My school shoes got the same treatment, and I was proud of the oxblood gleam I produced on my walking-out shoes. Being in the cadets was a blessing in the winter months because we were issued a navy-blue wool topcoat, which was much warmer than anything I had at home. I was always smartly turned out in my cadet's uniform when I attended regular cadet nights, extra band practices and weekend parades.

After leaving school to become an apprentice, I earned a small wage, which was added to the housekeeping money. My mother would then return a few pence, most of which I spent on buying cigarettes. I may have started by smoking cheap Grand Pasha cigarettes and then graduating to Park Drive and Woodbines, but now, I could afford Capstan Full Strength! Every weekend, I walked into town to shop at Woolworth where I always bought the same thing — a tie. The store tie counter displayed dozens of ties in all colours and all designs. However, I always chose a tie with diagonal stripes! Over time I amassed lots of striped ties.

I never really learned to save money; I spent it as fast as I got it — mostly on cigarettes. There was never any encouragement at home to save money. Although my father was a hard worker and earned a good wage, he rarely gave my mother much housekeeping money. He usually drank most of his wages at the local pubs on his way home on Friday night paydays. He rarely came home drunk, but having had a skin-full, he often became quite belligerent if my mother chided him. Invariably, he would start quarreling with my mother, always ending by his going off to bed, saying, "You people with your bloody education. You think you know it all!"

Most families in the area were poor and bought everything "on tick" (credit) — Buy now; pay later! Quite often, my mother would not have the weekly rent money, so my sister and I would cover up when the rent man called. "My mother is out today. She will pay you double next week," we would tell him. Sometimes, he would smile; sometimes, he would yell, especially if we had missed the rent the previous week.

I know that my mother made some housekeeping money by taking in washing and ironing, but to get extra much-needed money she often took personal things to the pawnshop. She was not always able to redeem the items, but then she may not have cared. However, there was one item she regularly took to the pawnbroker. My Grandma Goostrey had given me a solid silver pocket-watch chain and fob, which had belonged to my Grandfather, who had told her that I was to have it when I became a teenager. Each separate link on this heavy chain was stamped with a silver mark, as was the fob. I added two silver medals of my own which I had won — one for a swimming award and one for a bugle-band award. The chain spent more time in the pawnshop than at home. Eventually, my mother could not afford to redeem it and it was finally sol by the pawnshop. I wonder if that chain is safely tucked away somewhere, in someone's waistcoat.

I rarely had any extra money, but in the window of a local outfitter, I had seen a suit I liked, which could be bought on tick, with low weekly payments. The suit was brown, pin-stripped, and double-breasted with wide lapels, that being the fashion of the time. After trying it on, I agreed to pay a weekly sum of five shillings. They agreed to shorten the trouser legs for me. Even today, I have difficulty getting the correct inseam for my slacks. Instead of my overalls, wearing a suit and tie made all the difference when I dressed to go off to the local cinema. I also took to wearing a pork pie, although most of my friends wore a trilby.

Every Saturday, I would visit the shop to make my weekly payment. I was down to the final three payments, but that particular week, I found I was short of money and would be unable to meet my obligation. I felt I could afford to miss a week, just like missing the rent. I missed not only the first week, but also the second week and by the third week I was starting to get worried because I did not have enough money to make one back payment, let alone three. Soon, a letter arrived, which reminded me that I was in arrears and that I must immediately pay up my account. I let a further two weeks go by before finally getting up the courage to visit the shop. To my utter shock, I found that the shop was closed and empty, with a For Sale sign hanging in the same window where I had first seen the suit. While I felt relief, I also felt embarrassed that I had not met my obligations in completing the purchase of my suit, even believing that I was the cause of the shop's closing. It was an important learning exercise for me about needing to have both, a sense of responsibility and of commitment.

I wanted to buy a warm winter coat, which I had seen in a catalogue. The agent from whom you could order items was my Aunty Alma, who was a member of a club, which offered these catalogue services. My mother, a regular member of her sister's club, often purchased items for herself and the family. The coat could be bought on tick and I knew, as with the purchase of my brown suit, I would not be allowed to skip my weekly obligation to pay my aunt. The duffel coat I wanted was camel-coloured, with wooden toggle fasteners — the kind of coat worn by naval officers on board ship while at sea. Adding this new coat to my limited wardrobe allowed me to make quite an impression on my friends.

Wearing my duffel coat, my new brown suit with pressed creases in the slacks, my well- polished shoes and my hair combed into a "quiff," I felt I was quite the dandy as I walked down Great Portwood Street into the town center.

Chapter 8

GIRLS I HAVE KNOWN

A s WE GROW OLDER, many of us may think about our first crush, or about the girl who broke our heart. Hopefully, these past loves are happily enjoying life with a loving family and many friends. I sometimes reminisce about the girls I've loved before. In describing our lost loves, Willie Nelson best expressed the feelings of great joy and great sadness, often accompanied with the shedding of many tears, we have all experienced when he sang, "To All the Girls I've Loved Before."

I was only fourteen years old when I started taking notice of girls. I used to glue my ear to the radio listening to Radio Luxemburg and trying to hear the sounds of songs drifting in and out through the poor atmospheric conditions. It seemed that every second song was about falling in love with the girl next door. Nat King Cole was on top of the hit parade for weeks and weeks, his song telling us, "They try to tell us we're too young," but in the end "We were not too young at all." It was a time when most girls were just as rough and tumble as the boys, the only difference being that they wore frocks or skirts. The girls that I remember were not full-breasted, did not have long slim legs, rarely wore any make-up and barely showed any skin.

But there was Betty — the object of my first crush. Although sea cadets were an all-boys' organization, our commanding officer allowed teenage girls to work and serve in the canteen during our regular training nights. Twice a week, during the break between instructional classes, we would line up at the canteen to get cocoa and a biscuit from the girls serving behind the counter. There was much pushing and shoving and the younger cadets, of which I was one, would be elbowed aside by the senior cadets who wanted to chat up the girls. Most of the attention was on Betty. She had an outstanding figure and was often described as "the Bird whose knockers came around the corner before she did!" She flaunted her great body and used a lot of make-up to look older than fifteen. Even though her presence made my eyes pop, she was outside my circle in that she was not interested in a young lad.

Elsie, who worked with Betty in the canteen, was a nice, plain-looking girl who always smiled and chatted with us pleasantly while she served our cocoa. Over time, I began to think that she might fancy me. I wondered if I could pluck up enough courage to ask her to go to the pictures with me.

One night, I was given a chance to ask Elsie out. The cadets had just been dismissed from the parade and as I left the building I saw she was walking alone toward the town centre to catch her bus home. I caught up with her and, as we walked along together, we talked about the cadets and her school. When we had reached the bus station, I nervously asked her to go to the pictures with me on Saturday night. She said, "Yes." We agreed to meet in the town centre in time to catch the first show. When I told my mother I was going on a date, she asked me where I would get the money. I said I would run extra errands for her and my grandparents and hoped I would have enough to pay for our tickets.

I was so self-conscious on that first date that I tried to avoid eye contact with anyone passing by who knew us. While walking and talking on the way to the cinema, I yearned to hold Elsie's hand, but knew that would have been too forward a gesture on a first date. Because I did not have enough money for both tickets, we had to share the cost of the show; I did have some extra money my mother had given me to buy toffee. After the pictures, we walked across town to Elsie's house, not very far from the cinema. We said "Good night," agreeing to see each other again at cadets. After we parted, I wished I had asked for a goodnight kiss.

For several weeks, Elsie and I followed the same routine — walk home after the cadets were dismissed and decide which show we would see the coming weekend. It was always dark in the back row at the show and looking around you could see, in the half-light, that older couples were into some heavy snogging. One night, when I dared to put my arm around her shoulder, she snuggled up, and like the other couples, we snogged — kissed and cuddled. However, after a few months, Elsie stopped coming to the canteen and I was told that she had joined a girls' club, which held activities on the same nights as the cadets. Many times, away from cadet activities, we would all go out as a group of which Elsie was a member. We became great friends without having to make a commitment to my being her steady boyfriend. Leaving school to take up an apprenticeship changed my life in many ways, one of which was that we went our separate ways. Many years later, I learned that Elsie had become a very responsible and dedicated nursing sister in the main hospital of our hometown.

I had made progress within the sea-cadet training programme having reached the rank of Petty Officer. I was actively involved in teaching cadet classes, and my role as solo bugler in the band, also took up much of my spare time. Most of the sea-cadet band members had girl friends and together, we would spend much time travelling up and down the north of England, attending band contests and parades. It was usual to spend a Saturday morning travelling on a bus to compete in a contest in Rochdale, or Blackpool, or Brighouse, or Burnley and other locations in the afternoon, and then returning home late at night. Girl friends became our cheering squad and very often parents and friends, who travelled separately in their own vehicles or by bus, came to support us.

When I was sixteen years old, I was involved in the only sexual experience I would have before getting married. Every week, I went to one of the local cinemas, usually alone. Because some of the shows were restricted to adults, I tried to look older by wearing a clean pair of overalls of the kind that I wore for my work as an apprentice. I had no dress suit.

On one particular night, I was the only one sitting in the front row, stretched out full length, my neck craned back in order to watch the film. A girl sat down beside me. Although I paid little attention to her, I was certainly surprised when her leg slowly started rubbing up and down mine. I became aroused, as first her hands, then mine rubbed up and down each other's thighs. I can only think that she was experienced in accosting young lads, because she did all the leading. When the show ended and the lights went up, I tried making a move toward the exit, as I really didn't want anyone I knew to see me with this girl. A quick glance showed an older girl, neatly dressed but wearing little make-up. I guessed she might work in one of the local mills. But there was no escape as she quickly grabbed my arm and asked me to walk her home. Where did she live? It could be miles from the cinema, but I felt I could not refuse. A part of me wanted to find out what this pickup might lead to.

We carried on with small talk as she led me up an old cobblestone road at the side of the cinema. This road led up a hill, which passed through a large park area at the top. Only a few street lamps were lit even though it was around 10:30 at night. In the semi-darkness, she led me off the main path onto a quiet, grassed area where we sat down. Looking down, we could see the lights of the town centre below. I had never before been alone with a girl in such a situation. I found myself shivering with nervousness. I was scared, and uncertain of what might happen. She pulled me down to lie beside her on the grass, and putting her arms around me, began to kiss me feverishly.

I had often heard my mates talk about how they had made out with a girl, and it sounded so easy and natural that I thought I could handle it, if I ever got the chance. I had daydreamed more than once about what I would do if I were to find myself entangled with a woman. But a daydream is not reality! It was completely new to me.

Covered flesh soon became exposed, and the kissing and fondling became more intense, as her hands and mine found their way to places never before touched. She wore a corset, which I did not dare attempt to remove, so the struggle to get close was a challenge. What actually took place during that short time in that park, I really couldn't remember. After dressing, we walked hand in hand to the town centre to catch her bus for home. Before we said good night, she asked me to meet her on Friday night at this same bus stop. I said that I would and agreed to be there at 6:30 p.m.

I walked home, trying to understand what I had done, and nervously wondering about and fearing the outcome. I had heard that girls sometimes became pregnant after fooling around, as we had just done that night. My worries escalated when I suddenly wondered what I would do if, on Friday night, she brought her parents to meet me. They would know who I was and where I lived, and I would be the one to take the blame if the girl turned out to be "in the family way." I never followed up on my promise to meet her at the bus stop even though I went to the town centre that night, discretely hidden to see if she might be there. I never saw her again. To tell the truth, I cannot remember what she looked like.

Then I met a girl, who was to be the first true love of my life. Each year, the Stockport Sea Cadets would hold a two-week summer camp. In 1951, the camp was held in Scalby, an hour's march to Scarborough.

With drums drumming and bugles blaring, we would parade into town and down to the promenade to entertain the holidaymakers, some of whom were from our own town. It was usual for parents of some of the younger cadets to be spending their holidays there, as well as girls from our hometown.

At that time, I was seventeen and a cadet Petty Officer. My dress uniform included gold badges of crossed anchors, three stripes and attendance chevrons stitched on the sleeves. We may have looked like hotel doormen, but that did not stop our attracting the girls. One of the cadets introduced me to a girl called Margery. She was tall, brunette, slim, good-looking and neatly dressed. She told me she lived in Bredbury, very close to where I lived in Portwood, and that she was on holiday in Scarborough with her parents. Margery was seventeen. She had a friend with her, whose name was Janice, and Margery introduced her to my best friend, John, who was also a Petty Officer and a drummer in the band. It must have been the attraction of our uniforms, because before the band fell in and re-formed to parade back to camp, the girls agreed to meet us later that day after supper. We were both off duty that night and had been granted shore leave.

That evening, we met and spent most of the evening conversing, playing arcade games and going on the rides at the small fairground. Scarborough is a seaside town overlooking the North Sea and, as with many coastal towns, an ancient castle sits high on a hill at the edge of the town. Many people visited the castle during the day, or walked the paths around the outside walls, high up on the bluff. Except for courting couples, few people went up to the castle at night. At dusk, the floodlights at the castle were turned on and, even with the floodlights highlighting the castle walls, it is difficult to see any people who might be walking around the ramparts, even if they passed across the lights.

We left John and Janice on their own while Margery and I walked along the castle walls until we found a spot to sit down on the grass. In the shadows of the castle wall we snuggled, my arm around her shoulder. The night was warm and pleasant and, as we looked down over the town, a little kiss led to a heavy snogging session. I had no intention of trying any thing else because we had only just met; she was a nice girl and as my mother was always telling me, "A nice girl needs to be respected." I certainly wasn't experienced. It was getting late and we heard John and Janice quietly calling us to say that it was time for the girls to head back to their lodgings. John and I were free until morning roll call if we wanted to stay out longer.

Once we got down into town, John remarked about how dishevelled we looked. Grass had stuck to our clothes and our hair was disarranged! We managed a quick brush-down and walked the girls back to their lodgings. It was well after midnight before we reached Scalby. John was not impressed with his date and I think they spent more time talking than anything else; however, he said he would take her out again if I wanted to take Margery and make a foursome. We met the girls a few times before they returned home, but Margery agreed to meet me in Stockport when I returned. I couldn't wait.

During the next two years, we spent most of our free time together. I met her parents and she was introduced to mine. Most Saturdays, we could be found sitting in the back row of the cinema. She was my best cheerleader when we went to band contests, where I often won prizes for solo bugling or in my role as drum major. Our relationship grew and we started talking about getting engaged. We were never sexually involved, but even though we may have wanted to go further, our parents had always told us we should wait until we were married.

Margery was growing into a mature woman. She often upset me when she would tell me how well she got along with the bus drivers on the route she travelled to and from her house. She told me about one driver, to whom she was attracted. I certainly couldn't compete with an older, more experienced fellow. Maybe she did it to see how I would react; maybe she wanted to make me jealous. We both agreed to stop seeing each other for a while to see if our relationship was truly serious. At that time, I could not have predicted the change in direction my life was to take.

I thought a lot about Margery and wondered if we were really meant for each other. In the meantime, I met Joyce at one of the cadet band parades. This could only be a short-lived romance because she came from an affluent family, in contrast to my working-class background. She lived in the part of town inhabited by doctors, lawyers and bankers, but I lived on the other side of the tracks. She was stunning — great body, shapely legs, very good-looking with shining black hair slicked back like a 1930's vamp. I think all the gold braid on my uniform must have attracted her. I went out with her a few times but suddenly she stopped seeing me. Her best friend told my friend that Joyce thought I was nice, but that I was not fast enough for her. She wanted more, much more.

About three months later, I ran into Margery while she was shopping in town, and she said she was just going to get in touch with me. She had written me a letter, which was still lying on the sideboard, because she was hesitant in posting it. Marjory had met a sailor, a real HMS sailor, who had just finished his time in the navy and had moved to the North to get a job with a local engineering works. She and Alf had been courting steadily. He had asked her to marry him and she accepted his proposal. Alf was new to the area and he had no friend to call upon to act as best man for the wedding, so Marjory asked me to be his best man!

Indeed, I did act as best man, but I had no memory of the wedding — what I did, or even if I was there. An interesting aspect of this story was that a popular song of the day said, "I went to your wedding, although I was dreading the thought of losing you . . ." Even though I was left at the altar, we stayed good friends and corresponded over the many years since I emigrated to Canada.

While we were holidaying in England in 1996, my wife Yvonne, and I were invited to Poole to visit with Margery and Alf. In our discussions, the comment of my being best man at the wedding caused me to say that I didn't even go to the wedding. But Margery ran to the bedroom and returned, waving a wedding picture taken in 1955. With great glee, she said, "Look at that!" And indeed, there I was, looking very dejected as a member of the wedding party. Marjory and Alf have been my friends for more than fifty years. We were happy to help them celebrate their 50th Wedding Anniversary in 2005.

In the autumn of 1954, I was to meet the love of my life.

Chapter 9

A VERY SPECIAL GIRL

I WAS ALMOST TWENTY-ONE, FEELING I had been left behind in the world of romance. Many of my friends had steady girl friends; some were even engaged. All was to change in December 1954, when I met Patricia Taylor, who joined our office staff as our new receptionist.

Patricia was tall, slim and blonde with a peaches and cream complexion. She spoke quietly, often showing a shy smile. For several weeks, we just acknowledged each other as we traveled on the same bus to and from Stockport. Occasionally, we shared the same double seat. Finally, in February 1955, I gathered up the courage to ask her to go to the pictures. She readily accepted my invitation and we arranged to meet in the town centre on Friday evening.

We went to the Essoldo cinema to see Alan Ladd in "Shane." In trying to impress her, I paid for plush seats in the two and sixpence upper balcony and bought a box of chocolates. After the show, we walked through the town toward her home in Heaton Moor, an area of the town considered rather upper class. Coming from the "other side of the tracks," I wondered what she would think of my working-class home in Ashton Court. Before saying goodnight, we arranged to go out again the following week after I explained that my involvement with the Sea Cadets took up most of my weeknights. We continued to see each other on weekends, making sure that our growing relationship did not affect our day-to-day involvement at the office.

Several weeks later, for my twenty-first birthday on March 25, Pat surprised me with a gift of fur-lined gloves. I had never owned leather gloves before. For this special birthday my parents bought me a portable radio, which was seated in a very heavy, red and gray case the size of a small suitcase. I think the batteries alone weighed a ton.

In April, Pat told me that the family would be moving in June to Carrington Road, about a ten-minute walk from where I lived! Her parents had bought a small business — a news agency with a sub-post office. Bill was to be the postmaster and Nell would attend to all the newspaper and tobacco sales. Before the war, Bill had worked in the newspaper business on the production side. He had joined the army in early 1940, but broke his foot in training and was unable to join his regiment when they were shipped overseas. Upon being given a medical discharge, he returned to his job with the newspapers. However, because he had heart problems, he was unable to handle heavy loads. For this reason, he and Nell had decided to buy the business.

We continued to date, either going to the local cinemas on most weekends or spending the day out in one of the local parks. Sometimes Pat would attend one of the many bugle band parades in which I was involved, so I always paid extra attention to my uniform and equipment. She had told her mother, Nell, that she was dating a boy from work and that he was a bugler in the Stockport Sea Cadets.

But our growing relationship nearly ended.

Before Pat joined the staff at Hargreaves, I had always wanted to date Mavis, one of the secretaries who worked in our office. She had dated other members of the drawing-office staff, but had always refused my invitations. Now that I was going out with Pat and perhaps for reasons of her own, she accepted my invitation, when one day, I casually asked if she would like to go out with me. She agreed, but too late I realized what I had done.

That Friday, we met at the Super Cinema to see a movie. I was quite relieved when we were seated in the back row in the darkened cinema because I was afraid that someone who knew us might see us together. I had bought a box of Maltesers, which are round sweets about the size of small gob-stoppers made with honeycomb centers and chocolate shells. During the movie, I offered Mavis the opened box of chocolates; I had handed it to her upside down and all the chocolates spilled out onto the floor of the cinema. The chocolates rolled on the sloping floor toward the screen with a steady, rattling action loud enough to waken the dead! While walking home, after I took Mavis to her bus stop, I agonized as to how I was going to face Pat, certain that she knew about my date with Mavis.

On Monday, I got the cold shoulder from Pat. I presumed that Mavis had told her about our date hoping to make Pat jealous even though I knew that Mavis really didn't fancy me. Pat's parents had wanted to meet me, but after my date with Mavis, Pat told her mother she had decided not to see me anymore. After several days of not being able to think of anything but losing Pat, I went round to the shop and asked to see her, even though I had never met her parents. On that Saturday morning, I stood outside making sure that the shop was empty of customers before I introduced myself to her father, Bill, who was working on the Post Office counter. He invited me to step into the living room where he introduced me to Pat's mother, who asked me if I would like to wait until Pat returned from shopping in town.

Pat was very surprised to see me when she walked into the living room. With much embarrassment, I explained my actions and fully apologized. Fortunately, she accepted my explanation, but added that she was only interested in a casual relationship until she felt she could trust me. I think it was a defining moment in my life in that I finally grew up and faced the reality of making a commitment. More than once over the years, Pat told me that if her parents had not invited me in that day, she never again would have dated me. As time went on, I became a firm favourite of her parents because I think they looked on me as the son they never had. I also developed a warm relationship with her grandmother.

Pat's parents owned a car, but Bill did not do much driving at night because of his heart condition; being a qualified driver, I was able to take Bill up to his local pub, The Nursery Inn, where he lawn bowled once a week. Pat and I continued dating — usually going to the pictures on Friday nights, or attending a dance at a local club. Most Sundays, we would walk in the local park with the family dog, Trina, a full-grown Alsatian. He was so big that when he stood on his rear legs putting his front paws on my shoulders, his head was above mine.

Pat was very interested in my sea-cadet activities, regularly attending band contests. Parents of the cadets often hired a bus for supporters to follow our band to a contest. On one occasion, Pat's parents were in attendance and I had the opportunity to introduce my mother and father to them. In 1956, her parents asked me if I would like to go on holiday with them to Newquay in Cornwall. Since I had never been anywhere other than to northern sea cadet camps, I was pleased to go with them for a week's holiday that summer. The beaches in most seaside towns in the north are wide, flat areas where the tide gently rolls in and out;

however, the swells and breakers on the Newquay beach roll in with
great force. High cliffs, making it a challenge to climb down to the sand,
also guard the beach along that coast. We waded in the tidal pools
and fished for crabs, having a wonderful time being alone and at times
snogging in the seclusion of the cracks and crevasses in the rocks.

The following year, I was again invited to go with the family to
Jersey in the Channel Islands. It was the first time I had ever flown
in a plane, and I was concerned that I might get airsick; but the flight
was smooth and calm, much to my relief. Jersey was certainly different
from Newquay, but not unlike the northern beaches with which I was
familiar. Because we did not have a car, Pat and I walked everywhere;
we explored the quaint villages and the surrounding areas close to the
village where we were staying. In spending so much time together, our
relationship only strengthened.

Two years later, Pat told me she was leaving Hargreaves. She had
decided to work in the Post Office to help ease her father's workload as
he was in poor health and needed her assistance. I was now attending
night school, studying for my national certificate courses, so that I rarely
saw Pat. On the evenings when I attended night school, I made brief
visits after classes to see her. Often, it was well after eleven o'clock when
I finally left so Bill could lock up for the night. Most nights, we would
stand in the shop with only the streetlights for illumination, snogging
and talking about our future together. Then I would slip out quickly as
Pat locked the door behind me.

One night, I almost got arrested! Because it was a night-school
evening, I was carrying my brief case. I had just left Pat about five
minutes before turning onto Great Portwood Street, and it was then
that a police car quickly pulled up alongside me. A constable jumped
out and asked me where I had been and wanted to know what was in
the brief case. He said that a neighbour had been looking out of the
window at the time I had left the shop, and saw me slip out of the door.
After checking my case and noting my name and address, the police
accepted my explanation; however, the constable went back to the shop
to check out my story. Thereafter, every time I left the shop late at night,
Pat would always switch on the light as I left and wait until I was well
on my way before locking the door.

I decided that the time had come for us to talk about our future.

Chapter 10

A DIAMOND RING — A WEDDING BAND

Patricia and I had spent every free moment together for the last three years and now I was ready to ask her to marry me. Her parents had welcomed me into their family, but I knew they would expect us to wait until Pat was twenty-one before getting married.

One day we traveled to Blackpool. While walking along the Promenade, we were drawn into a fortuneteller's booth. She said we could look forward to a long and happy married life with a large family — six girls! It's interesting to note that we eventually had three boys. Soon after, encouraged by the fortuneteller's predictions, I popped the question. Nervous moments passed before Pat said, "Yes" — perhaps surprised, or because I had forgotten to go down on one knee. For the next few hours we talked about the plans we would need to make for our wedding, until I reminded Pat that we would first need to get her parents' permission.

Bill and Nell were very happy to give their permission for us to get engaged, and we assured them that we would wait until Pat turned twenty-one before getting married. That weekend we went to Manchester to buy the ring. We gazed into many jewelers' windows and every diamond ring she saw brought a gleam to Pat's eyes. Finally, she found what she described as the most beautiful engagement ring she had ever seen. To seal the occasion, I took her out for dinner. There, in a secluded corner of the restaurant, I went down on one knee and repeated my proposal for marriage as I gently slipped the ring onto her finger.

Now that we were engaged, we talked about going away on holiday together. We got her parents' approval to go, providing another couple would accompany us. We asked our friends, Sam and Doreen, to join us on holiday. Sam worked in my department at Hargreaves and he and Doreen were seriously considering getting engaged.

We went on a week's boating holiday on the Norfolk Broads, a series of interconnected waterways or rivers, which widen out to broads (small lakes) at a number of points throughout the system. The waterway terminates at Yarmouth on the east coast where the waters are tidal. Holidaymakers can rent sailing or power-driven cabin cruiser boats, which vary in size — some sleeping up to eight people. Most are equipped with a cooking area (galley), and lavatory (head) and sleeping accommodation divided between the front (bow) and the rear (stern) for privacy. While the sailing boats moved as fast as the wind could push them, powerboats had an engine control, which did not allow them to go faster than five knots.

The Norfolk Broads waterway system is one of the most beautiful and serene parts of the country. Many pubs, tea gardens, and waterside picnic areas are located along the waterways. During that holiday, we regularly slid alongside the quay and tied up to sample the local ales and pub meals.

I remember a funny incident that occurred on the way back into the Broads after leaving Yarmouth where we had tied up overnight. Because the water is tidal and the estuary is muddy, boats have to carefully navigate the shallow stretches of the river. Just a short distance from Yarmouth, we came across a sailing boat sitting high, stuck in the mud. Many boat renters were not familiar with navigating a sailing boat or a powerboat having had only fifteen-minutes instruction as to how to steer the boat before they were allowed to take off on their own. And here was someone who obviously had miscalculated the direction in which he was steering.

As we pulled alongside the boat, making sure we were not too close to the mud flats, we offered a line to secure the boat in order to pull it off the mud. As we slowly went astern, Sam, who was standing right up on the bow, pushed the long boat hook into the mud to keep us clear. The sailing boat did not move. The line tightened. Our boat moved slowly backwards. Gripping the end of the boat hook tightly, Sam pushed steadily forward, his toes in contact with the boat and his body almost horizontal to the water. Somehow he managed not to fall into the water, or to finish stranded on a pole in the mud flats. We were able to reverse our boat and inch back to the boat hook, which Sam was able to pull out of the mud. The crew of the sailing boat removed our line, thanked us for the effort and decided to wait until the tide came in. We sailed off into the sunset. We were to go back to the Broads a few years after we were married, accompanied by our great friends, John and Maureen.

With our wedding day in 1959 approaching, we needed to seriously look at our financial resources. I was always too casual with money; I earned it but never saved very much. Pat took over the finances, as she was more practical then I was. Of the many things I thanked Pat for in later years was her monitoring our combined finances to enable us to save a reasonable amount for our wedding. Without her leadership, I doubt I would have had much money to get married, start a family, or buy a home and finance all the many aspects of our future life.

On September 5, 1959, we were married at St. Marks Church in Heaton Norris — a church Pat attended before I knew her, and which was close to Pat's original home. Dorothy and Doreen, close friends of Pat's, were her bridesmaids. Sam was my best man and Brian, another draftsman who worked in my department, was the usher.

I remember everything, and almost nothing about that really glorious day. I recall that I was so nervous after the ceremony that my hands shook while trying to sign the church marriage records. If Pat had not held them still, I would never have been able to write my name. At the reception held at the Nursery Inn in Heaton Moor, my nervousness was apparent in the speech I gave that went on and on!

Like all newly married couples, we thought we had kept our honeymoon plans secret. We planned to stay overnight locally and leave the next day for Tenby on the South Wales coast. After Pat had changed out of her wedding dress, we took a taxi to Altrincham to stay overnight. It was a very large, imposing Victorian house with three floors and an attic. I am sure we were the only people staying over that night but they gave us the attic room up four flights of stairs. There was an impressive four-poster bed in the huge, well-decorated room. Although we had heard all kinds of stories about wedding nights, we were both so exhausted that after a short but passionate embrace, we fell asleep. My best man suspected that we were staying there and quite cleverly had phoned to ask if anyone had tried to alter Mr. and Mrs. Goostrey's plans for their wedding-night stay. When he was told no one had, he explained that he was best man and would they please make sure we were not disturbed. Now we knew why we were given a room on the top floor!

After breakfast next morning, we walked to the bus station to catch our bus to Tenby, South Wales. We arrived to find we had just missed the last bus to the Tenby Country Club where we would be staying. With no taxi in sight, we had to walk, while dragging our heavy luggage. I am sure Pat wished she had not packed so much! At least no one knew we were staying at the Country Club. Or so we thought!

During that week, we received many reminders from home indicating that we really had not fooled anyone about our location. There was, of course, the arrival by post of the proverbial chamber pot with an eye painted in the bottom, packaged in a box with lots of confetti. It's a good job that we opened it in our bedroom, being very careful not to scatter the confetti all over the room. About midweek, a large parcel arrived, which turned out to be my drafting chair from the office. Had they thought about sending my desk as well? That chair never did get back!

There was something beautiful and gentle about the relationship we started that week. All the times we had yearned for each other and had held back really came into focus as we searched each other's feelings. It was the beginning of a truly remarkable and loving relationship.

On our return to Stockport, we spent a short time living with Bill and Nell before we decided to find our own accommodation.

Chapter 11

IN-LAWS

BEFORE I MET MY father-in-law, he had worked for many years in the newspaper business. He was responsible for maintaining the machinery, which controlled the flow of paper in the process of printing the newspaper. Because Bill was experiencing heart problems, he was advised by his doctor to make a career change. He and his wife, Nell, had always thought about owning a small business. They bought a Newsagents and Post Office.

Bill was the sub-Postmaster responsible for running all aspects of the Post Office – pensions, money orders, stamps, etc. The post-office business closed at noon on Saturdays, which gave Bill the afternoon to study the racing forms and write down his bets for that day's race. After lunch, I would drive down to the local bookie on Back Waters Street to place Bill's betting slips. Together we watched the races on T.V. until late afternoon. Sometimes he won. On occasions — usually big races such as the Grand National or Derby — I would add my bets in with his.

During the Christmas holiday period and on a day when the Post Office was closed, Bill asked Pat and me to go with him and Nell to a steeplechase meet at the Manchester Race Course. Having never seen an actual horse race, I was eager to go, so we accepted his invitation.

Although it was a cold, foggy day for a race meeting, there would be no cancellations of the scheduled races. A large crowd was gathered at the course and after entering the grandstand area, Pat and I wandered around watching the antics of the bookies as they encouraged individuals to place bets with them on the upcoming race. We limited ourselves to two shillings each way on the favourite. During the afternoon, we continued to place small bets on each race. We had broken even by the time of the last race. Then we decided to go for broke and bet five shillings each way on Lucky in Love, a rank outsider, which if it were to win would be worth twenty-five pounds. It was late in the afternoon and the fog had become steadily thicker so that you could only see the start and finish lines in front of the grandstand. The horses lined up at the starting gate and then raced off disappearing into the fog. After several minutes, two horses emerged from the fog frantically striving toward the finish line — one was Lucky in Love and there was no jockey on the other horse! Only two horses finished that race and only one counted. An extra week's wage came in very handy.

Bill's gambling was not restricted to horse racing. A good friend of his gave him a hot tip on buying shares in a South African gold mine. He was so taken in by the possibility of a windfall that he bought five hundred shares at sixpence each, to a grand total of twenty-five pounds — about seventy dollars at that time. Every day, he would check the value of his shares as they slowly but steadily dropped! I think they went down to a penny a share before the mine owners announced that they were closing the seam. They never reopened the mine. The shares are still in my possession.

In early December, about two o'clock in the morning, loud, incessant banging on our front door awakened Pat and me. I hurried downstairs to find Nell, in tears, standing at the front door. "Roy, come quick!" she said, almost hysterically, "I think Bill has just died. Please run and check. Hurry!" I was terrified, but I knew I needed to go. I had only ever seen a dead person in an open coffin at a funeral, but now I would face being alone with the body. I prayed Nell was wrong as I hurried across the street, up their stairs and into the bedroom. Bill's body was still warm. I bent my ear down to his face, listening for breath and gingerly touching his wrist to feel a pulse. There was no breathing, no pulse. I returned home to tell Nell and Pat that Bill had died, and immediately I phoned his doctor to come and confirm the death and to inform the funeral home. Needless to say, there was no more sleep that night, and it was not until early morning we told Pat's grandmother, who was deaf and unaware of what happened while she slept in the adjoining bedroom.

During the days following Bill's death, Nell and Pat were in no state to handle the Post Office, but they were at least able to go through the motions of getting the newspapers out. The Postal authorities arranged to send in temporary help for the week. I phoned W. Hargreaves to explain why I would be away from work until after the funeral. It took several weeks for life to return to something close to normal. Assisted by Hilda, a temporary worker, Pat handled the Post Office routines. Nell looked after the rest of the business.

Christmas was quiet that year. Nell asked me to buy ourselves a cine camera on behalf of Bill, who had intended to buy me that gift so that Pat and I could make a record of our first child — their first grandchild. Nell gave us each a genuine sheepskin coat, which she and Bill had planned to be their presents for our having the baby.

While Bill's death had put much emotional strain on the family, we were looking forward to a happier time — the birth of our child.

Chapter 12

START OF A LIFE TOGETHER

MANY OF THE RESIDENTS in the retirement park where I live have been able to celebrate a 50th Wedding Anniversary. However, many are widowed and will never be able to celebrate that "golden time." But my married life with Pat was "golden" in that the many years we spent together are now precious memories.

In September 1959, after a glorious honeymoon in South Wales where we strolled the quiet, deserted beaches, walked into the local village to window-shop and stargazed into each other's eyes across the table at meal times, we returned to Stockport to live with Pat's parents. Although we were welcome at Carrington Road, we often talked about having our own home and children but we agreed to wait for three years before starting a family. Just before Christmas, we found a one-bedroom upstairs flat in Heaton Moor. This flat had a large living-dining area, a good-sized bedroom, bathroom and an adequate kitchen.

We were looking forward to our first Christmas together. At work, I had purchased two raffle tickets for a Christmas turkey prize, and to my surprise, I won! I wanted to surprise Pat by not telling her about the turkey, but when it arrived it was so big that we found it would not go into our oven; we took it down to Pat's parents to cook in their larger oven. As a Christmas present that first year, I bought Pat a large cranberry-coloured brandy glass. We had made many moves over the years, but that glass was always carefully transported to finally rest on a shelf at my home in Wellington. Unfortunately, forty-nine years later at Christmas time, I broke the glass during the installation of a TV cabinet upon which the glass had stood.

We lived in the flat for about a year. Pat enjoyed entertaining our parents for dinner. At other times, John and Maureen, who were now married, came to spend time with us as did Sam and Doreen, who were engaged and planning to marry in the near future. Later that year, a house across the road from Pat's parents, owned by Pat's grandmother, became vacant. Grandma promptly offered to rent it to us. Now Pat only had to walk across the road to work.

Near the end of our first year of marriage, we decided that we needed a car. I used to do a lot of cycling in my teenage years having bought a tandem bicycle from my uncle Norman. However, the bicycle had a heavy steel frame, which made pedaling very difficult for Pat to cycle any distance as she soon became short of breath. We really needed to consider buying a powered cycle. Scooters were all the rage at that time because they were easy to ride, good on petrol and convenient for short rides in the country. John and Maureen, who were motorcycle enthusiasts, rode a Norton, so we decided we would get one. We simply could not afford a car! That summer, I took a motorcycle-driver education course and off-road training program. But our parents did not want us to ride motorcycles — they were too dangerous, they were too fast, there was no protection and what do you do in the bad weather? Pat's grandmother offered us money to buying a car, instead. We accepted her offer and a few weeks later, we bought a new Austin A35 van.

The vehicle had a bench seat in the back and plenty of storage space behind the seat. I cannot remember why, but we christened the van, Aggy! John held a driver's license as well as I did and it was not long after buying the van that the four of us — John, Maureen, Pat and I — would drive away for the weekend to such places as Derbyshire, the Lake District, Yorkshire, North Wales.

One sunny, cold day in early spring, we took a trip to Prestatyn, in North Wales. John and I decided to swim in the outdoor swimming pool located on the promenade, but how foolhardy it was to dive into the pool without first testing the water temperature which was about fifty degrees Fahrenheit! Shivering and turning blue, we quickly got out of the pool. Once, while in the Derbyshire hills during the winter, we had to melt snow in order to get boiled water for tea. Although we had remembered to bring our prepared picnic lunch, primus stove and tea-making equipment, we had forgotten to bring water.

In the summer of 1960, the four of us went for a holiday on the

Norfolk Broads. John, who preferred sailing, was a natural sailor who could also handle a powerboat. The waters of the Broads are tidal and naturally rise and fall a number of feet depending upon how far you are from Yarmouth on the east coast. Potterhigham Bridge is a local stopping-off place for most boaters. It is a very small bridge with a low archway, only large enough to allow a boat through, providing that the tide is out! It was part of the daily ritual to witness the number of valiant attempts by Saturday afternoon sailors trying to get through. Some got stuck; others could not even enter the opening! Trust John. He knew when the tide was right, and we smoothly sailed on. Even then, we had to tuck ourselves down inside the boat's structure in order to avoid getting injured.

One day, as we were sailing down the waterway, and while the girls were down in the galley preparing lunch, John decided to tie up to the shore. It was easy to jump off the boat onto the land, tie up and make fast. John smoothly pulled the boat to the shore; I jumped off onto the grass and promptly disappeared, only to reappear on the other side of the boat! What I thought was land was, in fact, marsh grass. Spluttering and coughing, I treaded water while everyone up on deck laughed at my dilemma, more out of relief than humour.

In 1962, the four of us went on a tour of the Continent. Our prime destination was northern Italy so I bought an Italian phrase book to learn some Italian. Most of what I practiced I have forgotten, except for one phrase — "Eco el meo Passo Porto!" We left England to meet the tour bus and our guide in Holland, where we enjoyed scrumptious, crusty bread and cheeses; drove on through Germany and Austria, savoring great beers and chocolate cake; and over the Brenner Pass where I had an opportunity to practice my Italian phrase. As the Italian border guard moved slowly up the bus, checking the passports held out for inspection, I mulled over the phrase in my mind. As I offered my passport and prepared to speak, he said in perfect Queen's English, "Excuse me, senor. May I see your passport?"

Our bus, driven by a local Italian driver, who was familiar with the twisting, turning, hairpin bends of the mountain roads, continued on its way through the Brenner Pass. More than once, as we looked straight down the side of the mountain, I thought we were going over the edge. The driver roared along at breakneck speed, blasting his horn as we approached every turn. We arrived at Lido De Jesselo, just outside of Venice. Then in Venice itself we spent a day sightseeing, which included going for a gondola ride. Since the roads and streets are all waterways, gondolas serve the role of taxis in Venice. The taxi rank is a backwater and the canals are open, smelly sewers; tourists splashed cologne onto their handkerchiefs to hold under their noses. We were seated four to a gondola. The girls sat in the rear of the gondola and John and I stepped gingerly into the front end; we felt that it would tip over, so we held onto each other. Who would want to finish up in that water? We sailed down the Grand Canal to the strains of some local tenor who, in a nearby gondola and accompanied by musicians, sang song after song until we finally got back to dry land and thankfully away from the smell. Pat and Maureen never let us forget that time when John and I sat cowering in the gondola, afraid that the thing might tip up and land us in the sewer. Some romantic evening!

Late one evening, as we sat together in a small café, we called over the waiter to order a snack. He could not speak English. We could not speak Italian. Using a combination of sign language and broken English I asked for sandwiches and drinks. The waiter came back presenting each of us with the largest open-faced sandwich I had ever seen — just one sandwich would have been enough for all four of us. Learning some Italian would have been useful. On our return trip across the continent we spent one night at a stone monastery in the Alps. At night, for the first time, we experienced sleeping under a thick, feather-filled duvet – so warm and sexy! We also made an overnight stop in Oberammergau where the famous Passion play is performed every ten years.

During those first few years of married life, we shared much happiness with family and friends. Together we were establishing our lives, but soon we would need to relocate and find a larger house.

Chapter 13

OUR FIRST CHILD

MANY CHANGES IN OUR lives had taken place by the end of 1962. The company I worked for had relocated to Macclesfield, and I now had a forty-five minute drive to work. Bill's sudden death had left us all in a sad, confused state and Pat's pregnancy was reaching its term.

Two weeks prior to the birth of our baby, Pat was rushed into hospital having been diagnosed with toxemia — a serious blood condition that required constant monitoring. On January 12, 1963, our son Paul was born. My first impression was that he looked like a little, wrinkly monkey! Later that day, I drove straight from the hospital to attend a party, given in celebration of his birth, by Sam and Doreen, who were now married. I was in no state to drive home after having indulged in much liquid celebration; John and Maureen bundled me into the van, drove me to Carrington Road, unlocked the front door and pushed me inside. I awoke next morning to find myself lying on the floor of the front hall. Fortunately it was Saturday, and I had the weekend to recover.

Although it was a definite advantage for Pat to be living across the road from the shop, we discussed the idea of moving to save me time in traveling to work. Then one day, Nell told us she was selling the business and moving back to her old neighborhood in Heaton Moor. Now we were able to considered buying a new house in the Macclesfield area. Sam and Doreen wanted to move as well.

The four of us went visiting housing sites that were under construction in the area; we were very impressed with the houses we saw in Congleton, about ten miles from where the factory was located. The prices were reasonable and within our earning power, so we decided to purchase a house; when we informed Eric about our plan, he tried to persuade us to change our minds and to buy in an area closer to the new work location. He told us that we might be able to get a raise in pay, if we would agree to buy in Macclesfield. Yes, we would. We got an increase in salary with the promise of more to come, and for the first time in my life I was earning more than twenty pounds a week—just over one thousand pounds a year!

We found a suitable home — a two-bedroom bungalow in a small subdivision located at the foot of the hills which ranged toward Rainow and across to Bollington, where Sam and Doreen had bought a semidetached house.

The living room included an unfinished fireplace, which I decided needed a stone-faced surround with a green slate hearth. I sketched a design, took it to a local stone merchant, and two weeks later we went to his shop to look at the fireplace and hearth. The pieces on the floor were laid out like a large jigsaw puzzle. We were thrilled with the results — a brilliant array of browns, greens, mauves and blues — but we had to transport all the stones to our living room. I sketched the full layout showing the position of every stone, each of which I numbered, both on the sketch and on the individual stones. Some of the stones had been cut from old, discarded gravestones! It took two weeks to position and mortar all the pieces in place. After I added the green slate hearth and a solid wooden mantle, the finished fireplace stood four feet high, twelve feet wide, and included small and large recesses for decorative display pieces. However, there was a problem. Whenever we lit a fire, much of the smoke curled into the living room. The predominant winds, coming from the hills, caused a downdraft effect that swept down into our community. Adding a special chimney cowling, which ensured the wind would create an updraft, solved the problem.

We loved our new life in Macclesfield and spent time making our home attractive. Because I worked at a company that manufactured turf maintenance machinery, it was important that we have one of the best front lawns in the road. We planted rose bushes in the front yard — a typical English garden — and our back yard became a kitchen garden with a play area for Paul. We became great friends with George and Barbara, our next-door neighbors, who were a little older than we were. They had no children, but they loved Paul and would often babysit for us. Sadly, some years later, Barbara was to lose her leg from a shotgun blast during a robbery attempt at a sub-post office, which they owned. Across the street lived a young lady doctor and her husband, whose son was born on the same day as Paul. Both Paul and Tony, his playmate, were very active and more than once escaped from the garden while playing together. Then I would have to chase after them to get them back home. Paul's hyperactivity sometimes showed in strange ways. At times he would suddenly bend over and, putting his hands flat on the floor, would walk on all fours!

In 1965, we went to Scarborough for our holiday with our longtime friends, Ron and Beryl Jones and their daughter, Shirley. Ron had been a drummer with the sea-cadet band and Beryl had worked at Hargreaves. We stayed at a Butlin's Holiday Camp where Beryl and Pat decided to enter the children in the mother and child contest. Paul was quite chubby, his hair sticking out like a porcupine; Shirley was a quiet, little princess. They made a pair like Beauty and the Beast! Neither of them won a prize.

Although we had moved from Stockport, we had kept in close touch with our families. On most weekends, we visited with Nell and Pat's grandmother, my mother and father, my sister, Audrey and my niece,Tracy.

Little did Pat and I realize that in the following year, we would be relocating to another country.

Chapter 14

STEPPING INTO THE UNKNOWN

T HE CHARTER OF FREEDOM and Rights gives all new immigrants to Canada an opportunity to become citizens of this great country. From the early days of the twentieth century, European immigrants who arrived in this country worked hard to become conversant with the language and adjusted their lives into accepting the new culture. Many retained and practised their cultural heritage, but foremost, their loyalty was to Canada. Today, I feel that it is incumbent upon new immigrants in becoming citizens of Canada, to accept all the laws of the land and learn English or French, the languages of communication, in addition to maintaining their native tongue and culture. This is a land of freedom and opportunity. We must all work together to maintain all that this great country offers.

During the early part of 1965, two factors were considered in my reasons for emigrating.

First, I became very discouraged with my role in the company structure at W. Hargreaves and Sons. A new chief designer was to be employed to oversee my department, causing me to give serious thought to leaving the company for which I had worked for seventeen years. Secondly, I had a desire to join the many hundreds of emigrants who were leaving to start a new life in Australia, New Zealand or Canada. These countries were looking for workers to develop their vibrant economies.

I started my employment with W. Hargreaves and Co as a junior draftsman and, over a period of seven years, became fully qualified. I also developed an aptitude for mechanical designing. Chief Designer

Eric Staniforth found that I had the skill and talent to perform my work successfully and under his guidance I learned to perform all aspects of managing and supervising a drawing office. As I matured, I was given more and more responsibility and eventually I found myself teaching and guiding the junior draftsmen. I was told that, in time, I would be appointed to the position of Chief Draftsman.

I learned that Eric was to be promoted to Technical Director in charge of all engineering departments, and I believed that I would then become the new Chief Draftsman whenever his appointment took place. However, it was not Eric who made the decision to hire a new senior designer outside the company; Mr. Derek (Hargreaves), the owner, had made the new appointment. Even though Eric recommended me highly for the position, the new appointment was confirmed.

This appointment gave rise to our giving much thought and discussion to the idea of emigrating, particularly to Australia. We made an application and were delighted to receive approval allowing us to emigrate once I had an approved job offer. I applied to an Australian company for a position as a design draftsman in my field of expertise and soon received notice to attend an interview to be held in Manchester. We were quite surprised at the speed with which events were happening and this urgency caused us to pause and reconsider our decision to leave. Was it the right thing for us to do? Would we be happy with the change? What about the family we were leaving behind? Could we sell our house? How would I approach telling my boss that I was leaving?

But first, I had to attend the scheduled interview for a drafting position. During the discussion, I was told that I had the credentials and experience to be considered for a number of placements. Following the interview, I was informed that I would receive notification within a few days. However, before leaving the interview, I was asked if I would consider emigration to Canada. I thanked the interviewer for this information but told him that I would need to involve my wife in making the decision to emigrate to Canada. I was asked to respond within the week, but we had been so engrossed in preparing to leave for Australia that we had never considered Canada. As I made my way home that day, my thoughts whirled about, taking me along a trail that led me to North America, Canada, the USA, Hollywood! What an opportunity!

Pat's reaction about going to Canada instead of to Australia was very much different. "Canada is all ice and snow," she said. "If we go to

Canada, I would prefer to go to Vancouver." She was well aware that Vancouver was "quite English"— afternoon teas and scones! However, she did know that a specific offer of employment would determine where we would locate. The decision was somewhat decided after we looked at a map of the world and saw that it was much closer to travel to Canada than to Australia; it would be cheaper and quicker to return if things did not work out for us. However, while we never expected the streets to be paved with gold wherever we emigrated, we made a firm commitment to remain in the chosen country for a period of at least five years.

I contacted and informed the interviewer in Manchester that we were willing to go to Canada and shortly thereafter, I received an offer to work for a design company in Toronto. We were able to fast track our application since we had already completed the process for emigration to Australia. We agreed to plan for a departure in early April 1966.

Throughout the weeks before our departure, we kept our families aware of the changing situation. My father had passed away two years ago and, since her divorce, my sister was living with my mother, providing her with care and support. My mother encouraged us in our plans to go abroad, saying we should take this opportunity to start a new life for ourselves. My mother-in-law, Nell, was looking after her mother, who had been bedridden for quite some time and it was thought that she would not live to see Christmas. Nell had been alone since Bill had passed away, and we were concerned that after grandma died, Nell would be alone, unable to cope on her own. She asked that we not worry about her and that we continue with our emigration plans.

Two years before our plan to emigrate arose we had bought our first house, a small bungalow located in the foothills of Hurdsfield, Macclesfield and about two miles from where I worked. We loved the house, but once we had made the firm decision to depart England and had received approval to emigrate, we put the house on the market. We crossed our fingers and hoped that it would sell in the next three months leading up to our departure.

Brendon, our new Chief Designer, started his employment with the company in January. In the beginning, he worked closely with me and relied on my experience to outline the various roles and formats used within the design and drawing office. Eric was still associated with the design side of the office, but it was apparent that he was slowly handing the reins over to Brendon.

Although Brendon was an experienced engineer with sound design talents, I soon began to see that there would be problems working with him. I was successful at my design job because I had learned from working with Eric how to produce sound design with minimum costs. He always used to say that anyone can design a solution to a problem but the skill lay in the economy of producing it. Herein lay Brendon's problem and eventual downfall. His design solutions were good, but usually elaborate and costly; although I suggested changes to his designs, he would usually turn them down. Brendon would show and explain the designed product for the approval of the Managing Director, Mr. Derek, who was left no choice but to accept it. After all, he had hired the new Chief Designer. I could not help noticing that Eric was starting to get quite frustrated with the designs coming out of the office.

`To add to Eric's concerns, I informed him in a private meeting that I was emigrating to Canada and had accepted a position with a firm in Toronto. The last thing he expected to hear was that I was leaving the company and he began to give me lots of reasons for changing my mind. We spent most of the morning talking during which he even asked me if it had anything to do with the way Brendon ran the office. I admitted that I was disturbed by the way the product designs were changing and the lack of encouragement Brendon gave to his staff. I also felt that he undermined my role in the design office. Despite his wanting me to stay on, I asked him to accept a month's notice, as I would be leaving at the end of March. I said that I wanted to ensure the drawing office would run smoothly when I left, especially with the changes that had taken place.

We had kept the sale of the house quiet because we were still in the planning stages for emigration; fortunately, the house sold early in January and we agreed to close the sale at the end of March. Sadly, Pat's grandma passed away in February. We were quite concerned for Nell's welfare, but she assured us that she now had no worries, as it was a relief that her mother had passed away. She knew that we had all the plans in place for our emigration and she told us that we must follow them through. So both our families accepted our decision to leave the country at the end March.

It was hard to leave behind the house we loved. I cut the grass and watered the budding roses. Some personal items and furniture that we decided to keep had been packed and sent to Canada by sea and would arrive after we got there. Nell offered to buy our car. We stayed with her until we left on April 6, 1966.

It was a tearful farewell as we left Manchester Airport that day. It was snowing when we touched down in Toronto!

Chapter 15

COULD I BECOME A TEACHER?

RECENTLY, I READ AN article in the *Toronto Star* headed with this title: "Teaching rewarding, but jobs now scarcer." The story opened by asking a first-year Junior High School teacher if he had made a good career choice. "Am I making a difference? Definitely," he said. "It's the greatest profession."

His words made me stop and think about how I got involved in this greatest profession, and why I spent more than twenty-three years teaching technical subjects to high school students in the Ontario school system.

In the early 1960's, in my position as chief draftsman at W. Hargreaves and Son, one of my duties included teaching the junior draftsmen the skills and knowledge, which they would need to become qualified. I found that I enjoyed teaching and could communicate well with people who were eager to learn. I had always wanted to be a schoolteacher, but I knew that my family commitments would not allow my taking the time and expense to pursue a four-year course in England.

Upon emigration to Canada, I was hired to work as a design draftsman with a company in Rexdale, Ontario. The work was challenging and I spent most of my time alone, working on my design problems. Pat spent her days looking after Paul, our three-year-old son, and when I arrived home in the evening, she went off to work at a part-time job in a local convenience store. Pat needed to work because, when we arrived in Canada in the 60's, there were no government handouts for immigrants and we had to live on our savings. Fortunately, we were able to rent an apartment close to where I worked. Although we had not fully furnished the apartment, we had enough basic needs to make a comfortable home.

Each night, after putting Paul to bed, I would read the newspaper, trying to become familiar with the Canadian way of life about such topics as the political scene, the prices of goods and general stories from across the country. Although I was happy with the work I was doing, I was always curious as to what jobs were being advertised in the employment ad section.

One evening, a particular ad caught my attention. The advertisement asked for a draftsman, who would be interested in teaching, to apply to Prince Edward Collegiate Institute for an interview. It would probably amount to nothing, but it was worth a telephone call. Though it was early evening, the school's business administrator, who just happened to be in the school at that hour, answered the call. I told him that I was very interested in the information and could he give me further details.

It was obvious that with my North England accent, I was a new arrival to the country. He asked me where I had lived in England and then surprised me by saying that he was originally from Congelton, only a few miles from where we had lived in Macclesfield. He gave me a broad outline of the Technical Education programs being offered in high schools across Ontario. The Ministry of Education for Ontario had seen the need for students to become skilled workers through studying in the technical programs, but few trained teachers were readily available. The Ministry was hoping to attract the required teachers from skilled engineers and tradesmen who presently worked in business and industry. He asked me to attend an interview at the school on Sunday at 2:00 p.m. to get a clear understanding of the requirements for this available position. The principal, vice-principal and technical director were in Toronto undertaking interviews, and they would not be back at the high school until the end of the week.

After thanking him and confirming that I would attend the interview, I realized that I did not know how to find the way to the school in Prince Edward County. We looked at a map of eastern Canada and I found Prince Edward Island. I looked back toward Toronto and mentally measuring the distance between the two places, I saw that there was no way I could get there by Sunday afternoon. Feeling rather depressed, I called the administrator explaining to him why I would not be able to attend the interview on Sunday. He burst out laughing, explaining that the school was in Picton, Prince Edward County, which was about a two-hour drive east of Toronto. Somewhat embarrassed, I agreed to be at the school for my interview on Sunday at 2:00 p.m. I hung up the phone and scanned the map to confirm my route from Toronto to Picton but not without concern about the traffic on the 401.

When we first arrived in Canada, we were shown around Toronto by acquaintances of friends of ours in England. They picked us up at our apartment and drove us along the 401. Suddenly the traffic came to a stop. As far as you could see, lines of cars stretched ahead along the lanes. There had been a traffic accident. Stop lights blazed on and off around us as we slowly moved forward, nose-to-tail, in order to get around the damaged vehicles. I decided then and there that I would avoid driving Highway 401, if at all possible. Pat and I had recently bought our first car, and my driving experience was limited to the local area where we worked and shopped.

I could see from the map that I would need to drive on Highway 401 east going toward Trenton and Belleville. I remembered all those cars on the 401! Looking carefully over the map I saw that Highway 2 not only passed through downtown Toronto, but also ran along the edge of the lake parallel to the 401. I reasoned there would be less traffic on this highway.

On Sunday, the day of the interview, we left Rexdale at 8:00 a.m., and drove down to Bloor Street turning east onto the Number 2. This was our first adventure out of the city so we were looking forward to a leisurely drive seeing the countryside for the first time. However, we managed to hit every red traffic light as we slowly made our way along the route. The day had become progressively hotter as we drove along the shore of Lake Ontario, passing through towns and villages and making our way to Trenton before entering Prince Edward County.

We drove into Picton at 1:30 p.m. hot and tired; the air conditioner had not been working in our car. As we passed the houses along Main Street, we saw the residents sitting in their rocking chairs, slowly moving back and forth under the shade of their porch roofs. I remembered all the movies I had seen depicting life in the Southern states — all that was missing were watermelons and mint juleps! There was little traffic, as most people had vacated the streets for the coolness of their houses.

We drove to the school where I met the Technical Director, Doug Baker, who took me for a tour of the school, all the time quizzing me about drafting and my educational background. Then I was introduced to the principal and vice-principal. To qualify for the position, I would need to submit my educational qualifications to the University of Toronto to get approval to enter the teacher-training program, which had been organized for new technical teachers hired directly from industry. If U of T approved my standing, Prince Edward Collegiate would be prepared to offer me an interim teaching contract.

After saying our good-byes to the principal and vice-principal, I introduced Doug to Pat and Paul, who had just arrived from a walk in the park we had passed on the way to the high school. He asked us if we would like to join him and his family for supper before we returned to Toronto, but we told him that we would be very late getting back to Toronto if we stayed. He seemed confused until I explained how long it had taken us to get there. He said that I had misunderstood the Highway 401 system and that the traffic was relatively light once you left the Toronto city outskirts.

So we accepted his invitation. He introduced us to his wife, Roxie, and his sons, Larry and Jim. The boys played with Paul, while Doug and Roxie conversed with Pat and me, giving us more information about the community of Picton and the County in general. When we were ready to leave for Rexdale, he helped direct me to the quick way of getting back to the 401, cautioning me that the drive would be slower once we got to Oshawa because of the cottage-country traffic heading back to Toronto. We expressed our thanks to Doug and Roxie for their hospitality, and after saying our good-byes, followed the directions we had been given which led us to the 401 at Belleville. It was certainly much faster on our return journey to Rexdale than it had been to Picton.

The next day, I submitted my education and industrial credentials in a letter mailed to the University of Toronto admissions office, requesting that I be included in the Technical Teachers Training Program summer course. A week later, I received an answer, which informed me that I had been accepted conditionally, upon the submission of a signed contract from an Ontario Board of Education. In meeting this requirement, I would then be included in the upcoming technical-teacher summer course starting the first week in July 1966.

Pat was very happy to hear the news that I had been accepted as she knew that I had always wanted to be a teacher. I phoned Doug Baker and told him of my acceptance into the course. He said that the Prince Edward County Board Of Education office would mail me an interim teaching contract and also send a copy for submission to the university. I was worried about explaining to the company, for whom I had worked less than three months that I was leaving to go into teaching. To my surprise, the manager was pleased to hear that I had been accepted. He congratulated me and said that I should not worry about leaving the company because they would not hesitate to let me go if they decided that I was not needed.

That day, I learned a valuable lesson about Canadian industrial relationships.

Chapter 16

FOUNDATIONS FOR TEACHING

During the seventeen years I worked in industry, I made only one change — I transferred from being an apprentice tool and die maker to becoming a draftsman. Unlike today, I was brought up to believe that you owed an allegiance to your employers. Wasn't that the British workingman's role in life? Wasn't that created by the 'class system'? Had I stayed on as an apprentice tool and die maker working for Bolton's Engineering Company, my retirement years would have been spent in reading the papers and drinking tea, or taking the dog for a walk, or working on a garden allotment, tending to flowers and vegetables.

When I decided to leave Bolton's and became a design draughtsman at W. Hargreaves, the same worker-employer allegiance held true. However, in the Canadian work place loyalty between employer and employee appears to be rare! After informing my Canadian employer of my decision to leave industry and take up teaching, my anxiety was quelled when I was told, "If we didn't want you, we wouldn't hesitate to let you go." When I said my good-byes to my Rexdale employer in the spring of 1966, I felt no guilt in my decision to leave to become a teacher.

Before leaving for the first day of classes at the university, I had carefully studied my map of the city of Toronto to be able to find the location of the university. As I drove along the highway, I was overwhelmed with emotions ranging from fear of the unknown to feeling the excitement of the challenge ahead. Was I doing the right thing? Could I learn to be a teacher? What if I failed the training course? Listening to a voice on the radio singing a popular song:

> . . . I guess it's gonna be alright.
> Guess the worst is over now.
> The morning sun is shining like a
> Red Rubber Ball . . .

I wondered what the "worst" might be and if I would overcome it!

I arrived with almost an hour to spare, surprised to find lots of room to park, and when I went into the building to ask a staff member where the course candidates were gathering, he looked confused and asked what I was talking about. I showed him my paper work and briefly explained that I was there for the Technical Teacher Course. He quickly pointed out that I was in the wrong area of the city. There were two streets in the city with the same name, and it would take me another fifteen minutes to get to Central Tech. I drove as calmly as possible to the new location and, fortunately, I found a parking space. With only minutes to spare, I raced into the building and found the auditorium where the candidates had been directed.

A crowd of engineers and tradesmen were gathered there, all chatting and probably as nervously as I was. We were asked to assemble at specific trade signs: welding, machine shop, electricity, drafting, automotive, carpentry, and electronics. There were twenty-four prospective drafting teachers at our sign. My fellow candidates came from all over Ontario and had varying degrees of talent and skills in the field of mechanical drafting. Many were highly skilled in only one specific area of engineering. The principal introduced his administrators and the teaching staff, and he explained that, while he respected our technical knowledge, some might find difficulty in becoming skilled teachers and some might choose to leave the course before its completion. We were allocated timetables of our course content, which consisted of classes held nine hours a day, five days a week for the next seven weeks. How many hours a night would be spent doing homework?

That first day was a whirlwind of getting timetables, textbooks and equipment lists, hunting up the location of our classrooms, meeting instructors and professors and listing the reading material and homework that were required both for the next day and for later that week. Driving home at the end of that first day, laden down with notes and texts and homework, I thought that maybe . . . "The worst was yet to come!"

That evening, after putting Paul to bed, I did my homework. That was the first of many, many nights that I would be up until two or three in the morning, grabbing a few hours sleep before starting off for classes about seven next morning. Pat was always interested in my studies and when she arrived home about 12:30 a.m., she would make tea or coffee and ask what I was working on. When you think that she would not get to bed much before I did and was up early in the morning with Paul, her days were as long as mine. Somehow, together we came through those first few weeks.

Many of my classmates had up to twenty years of work experience in their respective skills, but none of us had ever taught a class. To learn teaching skills, we were given a series of lesson topics that we prepared for practice-teaching to our classmates. Presenting a lesson on the correct method of "Selecting and Sharpening a Pencil" may have seemed humorous, but we had to seriously present these topics to the class. There is something unnerving about draftsmen teaching draftsmen; after all, they work in the same area of expertise. But there were advantages. You could guarantee a correct answer to any question; someone would almost certainly offer a point of view on which you could build and no one attempted to embarrass you or make you look foolish.

The topic of the first lesson I was asked to present was "How to Check the Straightness of a Tee Square." It really was a stupid topic because never again, other than on that day, did anyone I know in teaching present that topic to any class of students. Our instructor was quite brutal in the verbal evaluation of each lesson that was taught. He did not hesitate to give scathing criticisms of student-teachers' lessons in front of the whole class, but I felt such open evaluations were largely destructive to a student's morale. The instructor's evaluations of my lessons were generally quite good, but he would always add, "Your students will benefit from your presentations, but you will have to work on your accent in order to be understood." Later, when working with my own students, I was to learn that a good teacher does not criticize a student in front of the whole class.

For several weeks, we continued to work on the Course of Study Outlines, which covered every mechanical drafting topic under the sun. In our plans for these topics we attempted to justify: the topic, the method of presentation, the student involvement, the project (if any), the assignment, and so on. It was as if we were planning a war with supporting documentation.

I made friends with Ben Mattson from Kirkland Lake in Northern Ontario, and it was through him that I was introduced to a Toronto tavern one Friday afternoon. We had been released from class a little early — it was a hot, sunny day — and I remember that Ben ordered two beers from the guy who was walking around the floor with a tray, loaded with beers. Looking around it seemed to me that most of the men — there were no women present — had spent the morning and afternoon in the tavern; many appeared to be in a drunken state. While we sat slowly sipping our beer, we talked about the course and our feelings about eventually getting in front of a real class. As the conversation continued, I called over to the man with the beers and ordered two more drinks. Ben jumped up, creating something of a stir in cautioning me that I could not order a second beer until I had drunk the first. I was astounded and explained that I was used to the English pubs where you could have several rounds on the table at the same time.

At last, I completed the Course of Studies at the end of August 1966, and we prepared to leave for Picton after loading all our worldly possessions into a small rented U-Haul trailer attached to the Ford Falcon.

We left Rexdale to start a new life in Prince Edward County.

Chapter 17

STEPPING INTO THE CLASSROOM

EVERYONE FEELS COMFORTABLE WORKING in a known environment, especially when one has experience and ability. However, in 1966, I headed into the unknown world of teaching with no experience and little ability, but a lot of knowledge in the subject of drafting.

We rented a small house on Elizabeth Street in Picton — a five-minute walk to the high school. We familiarized ourselves with the area in meeting with our neighbours, shopping locally and touring the high school. I was eagerly awaiting the allotment of my classroom so I could get organized for the coming term. I needed supplies and equipment in order to prepare projects and lessons.

Prince Edward Collegiate Institute (P.E.C.I.) had space for only 1,100 students. However, a total of 1,500 was registered! With so many students, two overlapping timetables had been set up — one started at 8:00 a.m. and ended at 2:00 p.m. The other started at 11:00 a.m. and continued until 5:00 p.m. Construction was underway to accommodate this larger enrollment but, in the interim, two portable classrooms were erected alongside one wing of the school. One was to be my classroom. My teaching assignments began with my first class starting at 8:00 a.m. and my last class ending at 5:00 p.m. It was just like a workday in industry.

On Labour Day, sixty-five members of staff met with the principal, who explained the school policies and directives. Departmental meetings followed with department heads adding specific information for their subject areas. After lunch, the principal invited all staff, together with their wives and husbands, to share a social time. I was one of twenty-five new staff members hired to teach at P.E.C.I.

One of my classes was with 5th year students, who were studying science technology and trades. Most students were conscientious workers but many were always out to put one over on a new teacher. This class began at 10:45 a.m. just before the lunch period. The classroom door was unlocked, so that they could enter early and set up their drawings. One day, during the second week of school, I found them unusually quiet as I entered the classroom. Suspecting nothing, I taught the lesson. "Time flies when you are having fun," they say. No sooner had they started working on their projects than the clock showed 11:30 a.m. — time to clean up and get ready for lunch. They left in a hurry, looking especially pleased! After locking the classroom and making my way into the main school, I found out why they were so happy. They had set my classroom clock ahead fifteen minutes!

Don Clack, the Eastern Ontario Inspector for the Ontario Ministry of Education, had arranged to carry out an inspection of my teaching abilities. I was nervous but I ensured that lesson plans were in place, the assignment was chosen, my daybook — a daily calendar of class lessons and activities — was up to date, and that the students knew that I, not them, was being inspected. The inspection proceeded smoothly as I presented the lesson and then set the students to work. I hurried around among the students not only to assist them, but also to impress Don Clack. After the students had gone, Don evaluated my presentation and complimented me on my knowledge of the topic and my handling of the students. He suggested, however, that if I did not slow down, I probably would not last the year! But I was still going strong when a number of years later I worked with Don Clack, helping him to develop a curriculum for mechanical technology for the Ministry of Education.

Qualifications for getting a certificate included having to write a trade's test. This test, combining theory and practical knowledge, is required to confirm your ability in your specific technical subject area. In February 1967, I returned to Toronto for two days to write this test, which consisted of writing a six-hour broad-based theory exam on the first day and completing two practical sessions of drafting skills on the second day — also six hours in length. It was clear that most of my fellow candidates had specialized in only one or two areas of engineering and were unable to handle the tests because of the range of knowledge required. In several instances, some candidates even handed in their papers early and left. I was thankful that my previous work experiences had been very broad in application and my practical skills included the ability to draw accurately and quickly. I was to learn that I was one among the very few who passed both these examinations. Only one of our original class members did not return for the second summer course.

That first school year passed quickly and, as May approached, I was asked to prepare examinations in my subject area. I sought help from my department head, as well as other teachers in the department. However, Grades 12 and 13 students wrote Ministry of Education Departmental examinations, which were administered and supervised by staff members. Upon completion, the exams were dispatched to the Ontario Ministry of Education for marking and grading. Each exam covered an extensive range of subject material, and it was not always easy to ensure that the high school subject teacher had covered all the contents of study for the year-end finals. Teachers had to teach to these exams and help prepare students by using previous Ministry exam papers. While many technical subject teachers disagreed with having departmental examinations, they agreed that they helped to maintain provincial standards.

I had to return to Toronto University in the summer to complete part two of the Type B Teaching Certificate. We were no longer rookies; we were now seasoned teachers. We had experienced that theoretical skills of teaching was nothing compared to the reality of teaching in the classroom. We were no longer prepared to blindly accept that 'this would work' or 'that would not work'. We debated issues from the strength of experience and continued to practice-teach for our class members, passing on some of the tricks that worked for us. The previous summer, we had been given a winter assignment to design a teaching aid, which would assist us with a lesson presentation in our subject area. I had prepared a form of playing-card game to teach the basics of orthographic views, which had worked very well with my Grade 9 students. Class members presented their innovations throughout the summer and we saw many excellent teaching aids displayed and explained by each candidate

After returning from a summer session, I met the new teachers hired for the Technical Department: teachers for architectural drafting, automotive, farm mechanics, boys' occupation and girls' occupation. The academic departments also included a number of new teachers. The student body was still on a split timetable and my classroom was still in the portable located at the side of the school, but construction and improvements to the main building were on schedule. Finally in January, I was given a classroom in the newly expanded technical department of the main school building. We now had a technical staff of fifteen teaching a broad range of subjects. The academic wing had been expanded to include ten additional classrooms, an additional gymnasium and extended library facility. All through December, I worked on completing the layout and arrangement for my new drafting room, setting up the drafting boards and equipment and ensuring that all the necessary supplies were in place. No longer would I need to move from room to room and no longer would I need to leave the main building.

New Ministry of Education course curriculums now allowed students, in the senior grades, to specialize in subjects that would allow them to pursue apprenticeships after graduation. Independent technical subjects were still available in Grades 9 through 12. It was a learning year for everyone. We had become a larger department with integrated specializations and cooperative education classes.

I was becoming confident and comfortable in front of my classes. Doug Baker, my director, had given me the responsibility of teaching drafting in the new mechanical technology courses to the senior Grades 11 and 12. My counterpart, Herb, taught the machine shop aspects of the courses. But these topics were never taught in isolation from each other. At every opportunity, I would sow the seeds of a lesson on which Herb would build, and he would reciprocate. We played a sly game, telling the students some details of what the other teacher was preparing to teach, but telling them not to let the other teacher know. "Let him (the other subject teacher) think that you are really very smart and have already done the research." The students accepted the challenge; every step was planned, and it worked.

Over the years we were to gain recognition for our innovations and involvement in technical education, not only from other schools, but also from the Ontario Ministry of Education.

P.E.C.I. was ranked as one of the top Technical Departments in the Province.

Chapter 18

A TECHNICAL DEPARTMENT WITH MERIT

THINKING ABOUT MY EARLY teaching days at Prince Edward Collegiate and of the members of the Technical Department with whom I worked, I recall how each teacher diligently taught his special skills to the students. Believing in our expertise and following that age-old saying, "If you build a better mousetrap, the world will beat a pathway to your door," we coached our students and set goals for them that resulted in their moving successfully toward their future careers. I believe that this attitude is the reason that we, as a technical department, succeeded so well at P.E.C.I.

Throughout the early 1970's, external bodies such as the Ontario Ministry of Education, the Faculty of Education at Queen's University in Kingston, Community Colleges, as well as business and industry took notice of what we were achieving at the high school. Also, other technical departments around the province were interested in studying our teaching techniques. We teachers at P.E.C.I. felt it was important to prepare the students into becoming skillful workers in their chosen field in industry. In my classes, I strived to teach them to be knowledgeable in all aspects of machine shop and drafting so that they were well prepared for an apprenticeship in this field. But how did industry feel about our students? Had we done enough? We needed to inform industry of our students' training and capability. We needed to know how industrial personnel managers regarded our students; we needed to inform them of students' training and capabilities.

We knew that personnel managers and directors would spend little time reading a multipage letter extolling the virtues of the technical department of P.E.C.I. Therefore, Herb and I prepared a simple check off survey format to be sent to major Ontario industries – the Steel Company of Canada (Stelco), Dofasco, Alcan, Northern Electric, Deloro Stellite and others – asking them what they expected from our students. What work attitudes did they expect? What basic skills must potential apprentices have? What academic support was needed? We received replies from most of the companies we had contacted, and with this firsthand knowledge of the expectations of industry we were able to compile a profile for students to follow.

After the first graduates from P.E.C.I. had been hired by Stelco and Dofasco, personnel from these companies came to see for themselves what we were doing to produce such high-caliber graduates. They left, fully convinced that our graduates would meet their expectations. However, the steelworkers' union at Stelco complained to their management that students from the Hamilton area schools were not able to apply for apprenticeships because most students from P.E.C.I. were being selected. The Stelco management arranged for their union leaders to visit our school to see what was being taught in our technical department; they left, convinced that the Hamilton schools would need to make changes to their programs if they were to compete with P.E.C.I.

However, good things usually come to an end. With little or no work opportunities in the County, many of our graduates went to work in Hamilton; after gaining their tradesman papers at the end of the required four or five years, many returned home to the County hoping to get a job in the immediate area. Stelco and Dofasco found that they were paying too much to train these tradesmen only to lose them once they had qualified. By 1980, they stopped hiring P.E.C.I. graduates.

Many community colleges sent their student services' counselors to Picton, hoping to attract our graduates to their colleges. Though this practice is not unique to most high schools, it should be noted that Canandor College in North Bay was so impressed with graduates from our electrical technology program that, each spring, they would send down a helicopter with their counselors to speak to the graduating class. It was usual to have requests from other technical departments throughout Ontario, asking that their subject teachers be allowed to visit our individual shops. As normal with teacher visitations, a lot of teaching aids and project information changed hands.

The Ministry of Education made a series of "Technology in the Classroom" TV programmes for transmission throughout the province's high schools. P.E.C.I. was chosen as the school for presentation of a mechanical technology segment, along with other schools in the province presenting aspects of architectural and automotive technology. I was chosen for the drafting segment, but it was unnerving instructing students while trying to ignore a camera aimed at the class. The Ministry of Education series was to be used successfully in encouraging schools in the province either to introduce, or to reinforce their technology subjects.

Our mechanical technology students excelled in their studies, but so did other students enrolled in the technical department studies. Our automotive technology students, taught by Bob Fagan, entered the "Chrysler Trouble Shooting" competition. A student's ability was measured by writing a multi question timed theory test paper covering all aspects of automotive. Also, two students working together had to find and correct preset problems created by Chrysler engineers. These competitions were run at area, provincial and national levels, with the degree of complexity rising with each level. P.E.C.I. not only won at the area level and provincial level, but also once won the national championship in 1973. As well, our architectural technology students, under the direction of Gene Snider, produced excellent plans and scale models of house designs that were entered into provincial competition. In 1980, the Norris Whitney Bridge that would connect Belleville to Prince Edward and allow traffic access into the County, was being constructed. For years, Highway 62 had been closed for short periods throughout the day because the original swing bridge would often open to allow boating traffic to pass, so that road traffic would be halted until the bridge swung shut. My technology students obtained copies of the Ministry of Transportation drawing for the new bridge and constructed a large model, which was publicly displayed in the Quinte Shopping Mall. People were now able to envisage what the bridge would be like. The bridge opened in 1982.

The technical department was introduced to the I.A.P.A. (Industrial Accident Prevention Association) Safety Awareness Program, which allowed students to learn safety measures in all technical courses as well as safety at home, on the highway and on water. Safety subject content ranged from fire and electrical safety to applying first aid. All students were tested on the material supplied by I.A.P.A. and the scores were included in their overall subject evaluation.

As an incentive to learning safety rules, I.A.P.A. set up a provincial knockout competition between schools testing their students' safety knowledge. Competition started at the local level with winning teams moving to a regional level, then to the area level and finally to a provincial level with the top two schools competing for the championship of Ontario at the Royal York Hotel at the annual I.A.P.A. convention. Herb Plewishkies volunteered to be the coach of the team the first year P.E.C.I. entered the competition. He selected a five-member team from all the students who had written the original tests. To say that he worked his team hard is an understatement. For three days a week after school, as well as on Saturdays and Sundays, they practiced answering safety questions. They wrote their own questions from the material trying to best their fellow team members.

In the first year of competition, P.E.C.I. literally blew the competition away at every level. The P.E.C.I. team was so good that it only needed one or two words of the question being asked before one of the students answered the question. The provincial championship was almost too easy. Using this winning approach, Herb continued his success for three years; however, he was ready to hand over the competition to the next volunteer coach. Because no one stepped forward, I accepted the challenge.

There were always at least one or two student members from the previous year's team who were available for the current year, but no student had an automatic right to a team position. All technical students wrote the tests and all were eligible for a place on the team. I decided that it was time for a special team tactic.

We had always insisted that the team members wear jackets and ties during the competitions; however, at times the students got uncomfortably hot, especially since a number of the competitions were broadcast live by the local television stations. My team decided to dress in maroon long-sleeved shirts and white ties, these being the school colours of P.E.C.I. I also had special I.A.P.A. logo badges made, which showed the winning years of previous teams. My first year as coach resulted in our winning a provincial championship, largely because I applied the tested methods that Herb had used. Competing with the team that year was a student by the name of Mark Vincent who, after graduation, went on to university and eventually worked for NASA as a rocket scientist.

Over the years, we saw that other schools' scores were getting noticeably closer to ours. It was obvious that schools around the province had taken note of our strategies. In my second year as coach, the school team reached the provincial final for the fifth year in a row. Although we fought a great competition, we went down to a close defeat. This was the beginning of the end for P.E.C.I. teams in this competition. In my third year as coach, the members were keen, enthusiastic and spared no effort in practicing; but we were defeated in the quarter final, one step from a semifinal game at the Royal York. But maybe I was destined to go down to defeat because of troublesome issues in my life at that time.

Whenever I turned on the car radio, I often heard "Mandy" by Barry Manilow being played. It's a sad song about someone new, entering your life. Because I was applying myself so much to the team and my classroom obligations, I was rarely home. If I were not on the road with the team, I would be in the school practicing with the team. I was also working closely with the local I.A.P.A. secretary in order to keep up with dates and arrangements. That year, a new secretary had been appointed and, during our times together, we clearly felt an unspoken attraction to each other. Perhaps I was looking for a break from the pressures of my commitments; it could be that I actually thought about having an illicit fling. She did ask me to meet her for dinner at a restaurant in Trenton to talk over the upcoming competitions. I think I told Pat that I had an I.A.P.A. meeting that night. We met, had dinner and agreed, that if P.E.C.I. won the next round we would spend some time together at the annual convention at the Royal York in Toronto. For about a week before the competition, I felt extremely guilty about this meeting; at the same time, I felt an adrenaline flow that people must get when they anticipate a romantic encounter. We lost in the quarterfinal. I was never to get to the Royal York. In fact, I never saw the secretary again.

I have, on odd occasions, wondered what might have happened if we had won and I had met her at the Royal York. I never told Pat.

Chapter 19

MY THREE SONS

CHANGE IS INEVITABLE. WE grow older. The kids grow up, leave home and get married. We make new friends. We change jobs. Some changes, we are happy to experience. Some cause pain and create havoc. Sometimes family life suffers as we get caught up in our daily work routines.

Although my teaching responsibilities took up most of my time, I tried to include a social life outside of school. Pat and I played bridge most weeks and in the fall, we joined a local square-dancing group, The County Whirlers. As well, I was involved in the community in serving as a training officer with the sea cadet corps, in assisting the local scout troop and in helping to coach house-league hockey. During the winter months, I took Paul for skating practices on Saturdays. I could only stand and watch because I couldn't skate; kids from Portwood didn't even have an ice rink! For his age, Paul was quite fearless. Dressed in a helmet, sweater and hockey equipment he was soon charging up and down the ice as a member of the house-league hockey team.

Inevitably, some of these activities changed with time. Because the government integrated the armed forces and reduced the military budget, cadet organizations were given a numerical quota. Unable to meet their quota, The Picton Sea Cadets were disbanded. Thus, began my ten-year attachment as a scout counselor with the 3rd Picton Scouts. Pat began working part-time at Sears in the year Paul started kindergarten, but when she became pregnant, we thought it wise to stop square-dancing.

A few weeks before the baby was due, Doctor Hall told Pat that the toxemia she had suffered before Paul's birth was occurring again. As a precautionary measure, she would have to stay in the local hospital for monitoring. I phoned Pat's mother, asking her to fly over to help me with Paul and look after the house until Pat's condition stabilized. Because Dr. Hall believed that both Pat's health and the baby's were in jeopardy, the birth was induced. Michael was born on March 15, 1968.

We needed to move because our house on Center Street was too small. We bought a spacious house for $15,000.00 on Paul Street, affectionately named Pedagogy Avenue because several of the high school staff and their families lived there.

That summer, I received a call from the administrator of Loyalist Community College in Belleville asking me to consider teaching a drafting class during the summer to an adult retraining group. Was I available for a six-week course? Because I had no required courses to take for my teacher's accreditation, I gladly accepted the offer, as the extra money helped in buying the new washer and dryer that we needed.

As we had done the previous year, Pat and I resumed square-dancing in the fall. We enjoyed the fun and the fellowship, the exercise and especially the time together. Some weeks before Christmas, Pat told me she was expecting a baby and we withdrew from the group. We took the jokes in good hand about the strange way that square-dancing and pregnancy seemed to go hand in hand. Never again did we dare to participate in the dancing classes!

In early January, Dr. Hall informed us that once again, Pat's pregnancy was toxemic and she would need to be hospitalized until the baby was born. A healthy baby boy, Steven, was born January 23, 1969. Though we were not disappointed, we had always hoped that we might have a girl! However, Dr. Hall advised us that it would be unwise to have any more children. Even the minister of our church poked fun at us when he informed the congregation that we now had our own television show, "My Three Sons!"

Only ten months separated Michael and Steven so that Pat had a full-time role as mother and housewife. Although I offered support by spending most free time with Paul, who was attending school full-time, I also helped with feeding and changing the boys. Pat was able to relax during the day whenever the babies were sleeping. Some days they slept too well because I spent many nights padding around the bedrooms with one or the other of the boys, trying to get them off to sleep.

Because it had been more than three years since we arrived in Canada, we felt that it was time to visit with our families. We planned on spending the summer holiday in England where we decided to have Steven christened. We left in July, dragging three suitcases, carrying the babies and trying to make sure we were on time for the plane's departure. This was the worst experience of my life, which I vowed never to repeat.

We stayed with Pat's mother. She was so happy to see the boys and especially Steven, whom she was meeting for the first time. The next day we visited my mother, who was thrilled to meet Michael and Steven in person after having seen them only in photographs. She barely recognized Paul, now eight years old and much changed in having grown so tall.

The local children, who were about the same age as Paul, were intrigued by his "American" accent. One day, we heard a frantic knocking on the door. When we opened it, there stood a child shouting for us to come and help Paul, who had fallen off the bicycle he had lent him. I found Paul lying on his side, the bicycle wedged between his legs, but when I tried to lift him up, I saw that the inside of his thigh was hooked onto one of the uncovered steel studs of the seat. After carefully working the stud clear of his skin, we took Paul to the hospital where he was treated and released. He was a "walking wounded" for several days, but finally recovered with no aftereffects.

Steven was to be baptized at the local church in Heaton Moor. We asked John and Maureen, our long-term friends, and George and Barbara, our neighbours from Macclesfield, to be godparents. Steven was a very active child, often throwing himself around or rocking in his carrycot. One day, we heard him loudly crying in the bedroom. We rushed in to find him lying on the floor after he had hit his head on the turnbuckle of the cot. Within an hour his head had swollen so much that we rushed him to the hospital. After a series of tests, the doctors determined that the blow had caused a blood vessel to burst that was placing pressure on his brain; they considered operating to release the pressure. We thought we might lose him, but slowly Steven regained his health; the colour came back into his cheeks and the swelling started to go down. After a week in the hospital, he was allowed to come home and before returning to Ontario in mid-August, we were able to gather together our friends and family for Steven's baptism.

John and Maureen visited us in the summer of 1971. Always interested in boats, John spent much time admiring the plywood and fiberglass catamaran sections a teacher friend was building in the barn at the back of our house. Although he had never before sailed, this friend planned to journey across the Atlantic. In June, he transported the sections to the harbour where he assembled the catamaran. After running several 'sea trials', he resigned from the high school staff and set off for his journey across the Atlantic. We later heard that he had succeeded; someone had shown us an article in a travel magazine describing his adventure.

Over the years, John and Mo often came to Canada to visit with us. It always happened that, whenever they came, I was involved in some major maintenance house project — either painting the outside of the house, or renovating and decorating the inside. John was always coaxed into helping me, which may be one of the reasons they later started going to Saskatchewan to visit relatives instead of coming to stay with us!

Just about every year, Nell visited us, staying for several weeks. In December 1973, she came with the family to spend the Christmas holidays, visiting Walt Disney World in Florida. We encountered some hassle at the border with customs, because we were landed immigrants traveling on English passports; it was quickly sorted out and we continued driving south to Kissimee, staying in a self-catered family unit not far from Disney World. The next day we left early to visit the park. Because of the huge crowds, the car park closed at noon because, as it was later reported, for the first time in its history the park had received an excessive number of visitors for a single day. The lineups for rides and activities were long, and the boys were hot, tired and miserable with having to wait. Michael, who had a habit of dragging behind to look at sights, was suddenly gone! I thought he was with Pat. Pat thought he was with me. It was probably only a few minutes since we had lost sight of him, but with so many people around we had no idea where to start looking. We left Paul and Steven with Nell and worked our way slowly back the way we had come. We finally saw him, engrossed in watching an animated clown, unaware that he was lost. We were more relieved than angry or upset with him as we took him back to join the family.

On one of the remaining days of the holiday, we visited Cape Kennedy to look at the enormous rockets and spacecraft, and wondering at the science that enables them to be shot into space and to return intact to earth. I especially remember the many alligators resting on the banks of the waterways leading into the space center, and the armadillos running back and forth across the highway.

It was to be many years before we were to return to Florida.

Chapter 20

INTERNATIONAL TEACHING EXCHANGE

I HAVE READ AND HEARD about immigrants who are well-qualified in their professions, but who do not meet required Canadian working standards. Considering that I was educated in England, and even though I spoke English with a strong English accent, I would have thought that my English subject mark would be acceptable to the Colonials. Well! It wasn't. I was expected to obtain an Ontario Grade 13 English credit in order to continue in my teaching career.

I was teaching a split-shift timetable in my first year of teaching and, having available spare periods in my timetable, I enrolled in an afternoon Grade 13 English literature course. As far as I was concerned, I was just another student in the class but the rest of the students regarded me with curiosity. Was I there to check on them? The teacher explained that my English transcript mark had to be upgraded to an Ontario standard as required for my teaching certificate and that was why I was in his class. He did caution the students, however, that because I was a member of staff, I should be addressed as "Sir" or "Mr. Goostrey." I tried to keep a low profile, not wanting to appear to have special privileges as a staff member. I was there to work as hard, or harder than they would. Unfortunately, students who wanted to get the grade with little effort, marred the class either by being disinterested, or by their disruptive behavior. If it had been my class, I would have seen to it that the work was piled on, or I would have suggested they find a softer option.

I had never read Shakespeare before that time, primarily because it had not been required. We first read King Richard II, and then, in small groups, we acted out some of the scenes. I played the part of the King, speaking my lines with such a broad English accent that few of the students could understand what I was saying. By the end of the term, I believe the students enjoyed my being a class member as much as I enjoyed being there. My efforts resulted in an A+ grade, which allowed me to confirm my Ontario educational standing.

Because I held a Type B certificate and my educational qualifications had now been evaluated for being equivalent to five university credits, I was placed in Category 2 on the salary scale. I now had to teach for two years before applying for the next level of teaching qualification — the Type A Specialist Certificate.

In the summer of 1969, I attended the Faculty of Education at Queen's University, Kingston, where I took the first year of the Type A Technical Specialist Certificate course. In some aspects, this course was not unlike the original Type B courses undertaken at the University of Toronto, which included written assignments, courses of study upgrades and practice teaching. Much of the Type A material dealt with pedagogy and regular teaching routines common to all practical subject areas: skills' development, subject knowledge and safety. Now, however, we were studying technical orientations and applications as related to machine shop, drafting, electricity, auto-mechanics and other technical subjects. A number of teachers on this course had taught high school for several years, and their experience in the classroom allowed us to debate and discuss their successes. We learned much more than can be read in textbooks.

Professor Ted Loney headed this technical specialist course. Previous to his appointment, he had been a technical classroom teacher, a technical director, and also an inspector of technical teachers for the Ministry of Education. He was a man who believed that technical education needed to become much more closely aligned to industrial practices of the day. Hands-on innovations and experiences in the new technology courses taught at a number of high schools in Ontario were the way of the future, and Prince Edward Collegiate was one of the leaders in the field. During the second year of this course, I introduced my fellow course members to Critical Path Analysis — an industrial process whereby one can evaluate which production stages come before others can be performed. I used C.P.A. with my senior students in mechanical engineering analysis. Because of my success with teaching these techniques, I was invited to serve as an associate to Professor Loney's staff at Queen's for two years.

During the school year, the Faculty of Education at Queen's University would send their technical student teachers for two-week practice-teaching sessions. Under the guidance of their tutors, these student teachers first observed, and then taught in machine shop, automotive, drafting, electricity and carpentry classrooms. Student teachers often needed a lot of support and encouragement from their associate teachers, but some simply did not have the ability to teach. As an associate teacher, I found it difficult to tell a candidate that he lacked either the ability to communicate, or the knowledge needed to succeed in teaching his subject. Many of my student teachers tried to emulate my style of teaching, usually with not much success. While I was flattered, I encouraged them to develop their own styles. In later years, I met many of the student teachers I coached during their practice-teaching days. I was happy to see that they had become as successful in teaching as I had.

My specialist Type A certificate put me into a higher category scale. Not only was my salary increased, but also I was qualified to apply for a position as technical director in an Ontario high school. I was faced with a choice — gaining further qualifications, or advancing in my studies to obtain five courses at University in order to reach my maximum category. With all things considered, I felt the effort to constantly improve and upgrade my teaching skills was far more important than taking courses that have little or no bearing on my subject. I chose to put my efforts into teaching my subject.

However, I started to get restless at P.E.C.I. After six years, it had just become another job. Perhaps I was bored? I wondered if I should seek a teaching position elsewhere.

I told my director that I was considering moving to another school, and he said that, even though he would hate to see me go, he would give me an exceptional recommendation if I were to leave. I had read about a teaching opportunity in Jamaica. I sent my application and credentials and quickly received a reply offering me a position that looked very inviting. After carefully considering all that we had achieved as a family, we decided against the move. Knowing that we could be directed to go anywhere in the world, Pat and I discussed the possibility of my applying for an exchange teaching position in England. To be considered for international exchange teaching, you have to apply to the Ministry stating your preference for a country; your department head, your principal and your school board must sanction your application. Each application is matched with a similar international submission and, if a match is found, each teacher is advised to establish contact. In 1974, I applied for and was granted the opportunity to teach on exchange in Yorkshire, England.

Dennis Reid, my exchange teacher, taught at the West Leeds Boys High School. As well as acting as department head, his main teaching subject was woodworking with a secondary subject in drafting. He and his family lived in Ilkley, Yorkshire, which was about a half-hour drive from the school. The Leeds Education Authority would pay Dennis his regular salary while teaching in Canada, and I would be paid by my own Board of Education while teaching in England. At that time, the cost of living in Canada was higher than that of England, so the Canadian teacher was asked to pay $500.00 toward supporting the English teacher. As was quite normal on the exchange program, we arranged for the Reids to live in our house and drive our car, and we were to live in their house and drive their car. Both of us arranged to insure the other's car as well as paying the heating, hydro, and telephone bills.

In the summer of 1974, we left for England for a year of exchange teaching.

Chapter 21

THE CLOCK HAD STOPPED!

IT WAS 1974, AND we were on our way to England for a year of International Teaching Exchange at West Leeds Boys High School, Yorkshire. I wondered how much had changed since I had left a similar school system back in Stockport many years before.

In July, leaving Paul with me in Picton, Pat travelled to England with Mike and Steven to visit with her mother. She also wanted to meet with the Reids, our exchange family in Ilkely, before they left for Canada.

In early August, I drove to Toronto to meet the Reid family. Dennis was tall and thin, typically English in manner and dress, and standing out like a "sore thumb" wearing his Burberry coat in the middle of August! Stella, his wife, was a very quiet, timid person and appeared rather subservient. They had two young boys. We drove back to Picton and following a short tour of our house, we left them to rest and relax after promising that we would return the next day.

Dennis experienced a cultural shock as he was caught off guard by the pleasant, informal attitude of the town's people. For example, while we were walking down Main Street toward the bank where Dennis was to arrange an account, I casually introduced him to Don King. Dennis asked, "Who was that?" as Don walked away. I answered, "Don is the Mayor of Picton." Dennis expressed surprise at this casual encounter. We then walked to the local bank branch of the C.I.B.C. The manager's door was open and we simply walked in. After I introduced him to the manager, Dennis arranged his banking needs and, as we left the bank, Dennis said that he was taken aback at how I simply walked into the manager's office, unannounced. He hoped that I would not expect to do that when I got to England! Politely, I informed him that he had better get used to this casual way of life because that was how people behaved in the daily routine of a Canadian rural town.

Paul and I flew to England in mid-August, and after a short stay in Stockport, we moved to Yorkshire. The Reids' house was a large, stone-faced, two-story, Victorian-style structure built in the late nineteenth century. It faced upon a large park area through which ran a small brook. The local shopping area was close by. The primary school, which Mike and Steven would attend, was located on the main Ilkely-to-Leeds road, about a ten-minute walk. Paul, who was twelve, would attend the middle school located further along the main road.

The town of Ilkley is a popular destination for walkers and hikers who ride the train or travel by car from their hometowns on weekends to spend the day traversing the wild expansive trails. Ilkley is located on the edge of Ilkley Moor, made famous in the English folk song, which begins:

> Where hast tha bin since I saw thee?
> On Ilkley Moor bar tat
> Tha'll go an catch tha death o' cold

I arranged to car-pool with two of the teaching staff at West Leeds who lived in the Ilkley area. A week before classes were to start, I visited the school to familiarize myself with the layout and routines. I was introduced to the headmaster and deputy headmaster. My timetable showed that I would be teaching drafting, woodworking and industrial design.

I had been teaching in a progressive Ontario technical school system with new, up-to-date equipment and supplies. Ontario's curriculum closely paralleled the practices found in business and industry, so I was looking forward to seeing what strides had taken place in the English system, which I had left twenty-five years ago. I walked down the hallway of the school, and it seemed that the clock had turned back the years and had actually stopped! The worn, wooden floors were the same, as was the pungent odour of sweating bodies, which seeps into the woodwork of old school buildings. The shop equipment was one step removed from the Industrial Revolution. It was as if I had just walked out of Stockport Technical School for Boys and straight into

West Leeds Boys. But this was 1975 and not 1949. Nothing, but nothing had changed!

An assembly was held on the first day of school. The Head and his deputy wore academic gowns while other staff members were formally dressed. Students wore school uniforms — black blazers, grey flannels, white shirts and black ties. During his comments to the student body, the headmaster introduced the teacher from "America," who would be teaching Mr. Reid's classes. At the end of the assembly, the teachers lead students to their classrooms, all the while screaming and yelling orders. "Silence there!" "Line up!" "Get your shoulders back!" Because I had no class scheduled in the first period, I was spared this fracas. I was ready to teach when my scheduled classes arrived, but the students were only interested in where Mr. Reid was teaching and my background. Who are you? Do you live in America, or is it called Canada? Do you know so and so who lives in Toronto?

The students were convinced that I was American because I used many expressions, phrases and words, which make me sound "American" to people in England. When they talked with me, they imitated the western drawl they often heard in cowboy movies. At times I got annoyed because I never knew if they were just putting me on. My problem was that I found it difficult to follow their Yorkshire dialect. When I finally told them that I was born in Stockport, less than eighty miles away, had grown up, gone to school and worked there for many years before emigrating to Canada, they realized I was able to talk about things with which they were familiar — soccer, rugby, cricket and trips to Blackpool and Scarborough. They were not the only ones who knew what "snogging" meant!

They often asked about the Canadian school system and student programmes, and they were keen to know how Mr. Reid was getting along in Canada. Unfortunately, I had to make up a few stories for them as I never received any news directly from Dennis; however, I did get letters from my fellow-technical staff asking, "When are you coming back?" They complained that Dennis was not really fitting in with the department or the school. Maybe he was overcome by the casual and informal attitudes of the technical staff, or the relaxed attitude of the students. The sergeant-major approach wouldn't work for him there.

Many students were from ethnic backgrounds such as Pakistani, West Indian and Indian. They had difficulty not only with their schoolwork, but also with fitting in. More than once, I played the role of counsellor, or advisor, or father figure. These teenagers were a challenge to teach, but most were very loyal once I had established the ground rules. Every Monday morning, they would discuss the past weekend Leeds United soccer match. I quickly learned that the game and the final score were not that important; to them it was the "rumble" they had with the supporters of the other team. It seems that the game was incidental to that of having a good fight and getting a bloodied nose or black eye!

Time may have stood still in the classroom routines, but school dinners were quite different from back when they consisted of potato hash, greens, sponge cake and custard. Today it was different — curry! The lunch period lasted an hour and once the students had eaten, they were free to go out into the school grounds. I was aware that West Leeds Boys School was located next to the West Leeds Girls School, divided by a lane. However, the school rules stated that boys must not fraternize with girls — under pain of death! Keeping a check on all the students was a new experience for me because the boys, mainly from the Upper Fifth and Sixth, and in their mid to late teens, used every avenue of escape to get together with the girls in the lane between the schools. The younger students were content to play cricket and soccer, or just talk in small groups. At the end of each school day, as the ringing of the school bell signified the end of classes, a charging mob of students raced for the school gates. There, on the boundary of the school grounds, ties and blazers would be doffed and stuffed into satchels. Shirts would be pulled outside of pants. They were free!

Of course there were problem students, but I was able to handle them. However, a more pressing problem was not having proper equipment; teaching drafting is straightforward, if you have the supplies. There was little to work with — even pencils were few. Compasses had to be shared between students. Scale rulers were worn and gnarled. I talked with Nigel, my department head, about the shortage of supplies. Because Dennis Reid had failed to requisition supplies, an order had never been placed. I made up my mind to purchase what I needed from my own pocket. Any school supplies that would come in later would be kept in reserve.

I saw a number of examples of poor planning throughout my time at West Leeds; often I wondered how the students ever succeeded in their studies. Everything appeared to be in short supply, if at all available! The first time I had to run off some subject-aid sheets on the Gestetner I told Nigel that I wanted a number of copies. He asked how many I wanted, and when I told him I needed twenty-five, he painstakingly counted out the exact number — even sheets of paper were in short supply! Back in Ontario, I was used to giving aid sheets to students for them to keep for studying, but I now found that I had to retrieve the sheets in order to use them with other classes.

Each spring, West Leeds held a field day raising funds for school supplies and equipment as a means of supplementing the budget. Among the many activities was a dunk tank — students purchased balls to throw at a bull's eye, hoping to send a seated person into the water. You can guess who sat in that seat most of the afternoon! A stranger activity was the Donkey Derby. A double, circular roped-off racecourse, about a hundred yards around, is arranged so that the jockeys run their donkeys only between the ropes. Punters make bets on which donkey will win the race. Unlike horse racing, donkeys don't shoot out of the starting gate. In fact, some even go backwards, if they move at all. I believe that these derbies are held only in the north of England.

At the end of the day, after I had taught my last class, I always spent time cutting wood stock for the following day's classes. Students were restricted from using dangerous shop equipment such as a table-saw. I was familiar with all the safety measures, having been involved with machinery throughout my working life. I had also spent hundreds of hours working with school-safety teams in Picton, teaching them the safety rules of using machinery.

A parent-teacher evening was scheduled in mid-June. That day, as usual, I cut the last piece of wood stock and flicked my hand across the pieces to clear them away. My finger touched the running saw, and immediately, I could see that I had lost part of my left index finger. Instantly, I reached for my handkerchief to apply pressure and trying to keep calm, switched off the machine and walked into the next classroom to report what had happened. My two fellow shop teachers were panic-stricken and ran around in circles trying to decide what to do. I suggested that it would be a good idea to drive me to the hospital. As one teacher hurried me to his car, the other went looking for the piece of severed finger! The hospital emergency staff gave me a series of needles to freeze the injury and to offset the chance of shock. I was aware from the sounds that the doctor had clipped off the top of the finger bone before closing and stitching the cut. They bandaged the finger and released me. I could not feel anything at that time. I returned to school in time to meet the parents at the appointed times. Although I was told to go home, I really felt quite calm and decided to stay. During one parent interview I was asked what had happened to my finger. I simply replied that I had cut my finger.

I arrived home at nine o'clock that evening. Pat was in the living room, reading. I did not immediately show her my hand, which I held behind my back, but finally I said that I sustained a serious cut at school. When I showed her my bandaged finger and told her exactly what had happened, she was very concerned but relieved that I had not had a more serious accident. Later that night, the pain increased as the freezing diminished. I got little sleep and the following morning experienced some shock reaction. Pat phoned the school, explained my situation and told them that I could not attend school that day. The school administrator knew of my cut finger and told her that I should stay away the rest of the week and return the following Monday.

There is a humorous side to this accident. In the previous spring, before leaving for my year of exchange teaching, I had taken some guitar lessons. I had reached the stage where I could play chords to a tune such as, "Take me Home, Country Road." I practiced a lot, struggling to get calluses on my fingertips so the strings would not cut into them. Here I was a year later, with a finger that would not even reach the string! Like my non-singing career I never had as a boy, I was never to be another Glen Campbell or Willie Nelson.

The staff held a farewell gathering on my final day of exchange at West Leeds, and the headmaster gave a speech in which he recognized my contributions to the life of the school. On behalf of the staff, he presented me with an engraved pewter tankard. He did say, however, that he was glad I was finally leaving because he was not too happy to have someone on his staff who was earning more than he was! In the evening, the staff hosted Pat and me to a Mediaeval Banquet. We had a very enjoyable, though moving experience, as most of the staff came to wish us farewell and to say how much they had enjoyed meeting us. At the end of the evening, as we went to our car to leave, Noel, a fellow shop teacher, came to say a good-bye with tears streaming down his cheeks. He told me how much he appreciated what I had done, not only for the school, but also for him as a fellow department member. I also cried.

We have stayed in touch with each other ever since.

Chapter 22

SOCIAL LIFE IN YORKSHIRE

TWO MONTHS INTO MY overseas teaching position, I began questioning my decision in taking this exchange posting at West Leeds Boys' School. The lack of supplies and equipment made it very difficult to educate students to the requisite levels. While I accepted my professional commitments and tried to obtain the best results possible, I also realized my family was as important as my work. I set out to balance work, family and play.

Every second weekend, we would squeeze into the Reids' car and head for Stockport, crossing the Pennines from Yorkshire to Lancashire. The route took us through the city of Bradford. I was unprepared for the changes I saw since last I drove through that city. The street signs, the road names, the shops and the goods they sold, and the titles of movies were all in Pakistani, or Hindi. The streets were crowded with buses, cars and people shopping at the multitude of sidewalk stalls. On our visits to Stockport, we stayed with Pat's mother because she had additional space for our family, but we also visited my family and friends we had not seen since we had emigrated to Canada.

Visiting teachers on international exchange are invited to attend a number of planned events throughout their stay in the country of exchange. On one occasion, we visited a medieval mansion in the Lake District; on another, we took a steam train ride to Howarth, where we visited the home of Charlotte Bronte, famous for her having written the classic novel *Wuthering Heights*.

Prior to Christmas, a reporter approached us from the Ilkley newspaper and requested a family interview. He was seeking our reactions to living and working in the area. When the report was published in the newspaper the following week, we were surprised to find that another Canadian exchange teacher, Mick Stewart, from Dundas, Ontario was teaching geography at a Secondary Modern School in Leeds. He and his wife Lillian, with their two young children, lived a short distance from our house in Ilkley. Mick had been a teacher in England before emigrating to Canada. We arranged to meet at the Ilkely Arms, a local pub, where we compared notes on day-to-day living, school experiences, and how well our children were adjusting. We both confessed that we could not wait to get back home to Canada.

While I spent much time on preparing lessons, I did create free time to spend with the family. As a teenager I had always enjoyed building model balsa-wood airplanes, so I decided to construct one for the boys. It took a few weeks to complete the forty-eight-inch wing span glider, but the boys were looking forward, excitedly, to launch day! On the test flight day, my three boys and I carefully transported the model up to an open area of the moor, locally referred to as The Tarn. This wide-open space overlooks the town from high up and was perfect for launching a glider. After a few short practice glides it sailed up into the wind, rapidly gaining height as Paul, Michael and Steven stood watching in amazement. It was only a few minutes before we realized that the glider was not only rising, but also sailing gracefully down toward the town. We chased down the hillside after the glider, which finally came to rest on the lower slope of the hill. We tried several additional flights, the boys remaining at the bottom of the hill while I struggled to run up the hill back to the launching point. That model was far too big and fragile to consider moving it from Ilkley; when we packed to return to Canada, my sons left it as a gift for the Reid boys.

We had promised the boys that we would visit a village near Stockport named after us. They really did not believe that there was such a place until we arrived on the outskirts. There, affixed on a high steel pole, was posted a large sign announcing GOOSTREY. We wandered through the village finding the Goostrey post office, the Goostrey church and the many Goostrey graves in the cemetery.

Pat's mother offered to take the boys on the spring holiday to Starcoast World, a Butlin's Holiday Camp in North Wales, while Pat and I went to visit our friends, John and Maureen, who were living in Gibraltar. John worked for the British government as a maintenance supervisor of the harbour and dock. He was a qualified scuba and deep-sea diver, and when we visited him in his office he invited me to try on the heavy, solid brass helmet that he wore while diving. He said that the water buoyancy helped to relieve the weight as he descended into the depths of the sea. I tried on that heavy helmet but declined the diving experience!

During our stay, we toured the island, strolling along the streets of the fishing villages, sampling calamari and swordfish, watching the antics of the Barbary apes in the hillside caves, as well as touring the wartime fortifications.

When Pat came down with a mild case of chicken pox we were concerned that the airport authorities might delay our departure, but the rash faded and with the aid of make-up we passed through immigration. We arrived back in Stockport to find that Paul and Steven both had chicken pox while they were in North Wales. Paul's infection was more serious, so he had to wear long-sleeved shirts with high necks in order to hide the spots. Michael did not catch it. To our surprise the boys had been well behaved even under those trying conditions.

All the teachers on international exchange received an invitation to attend a royal garden party to be held in June at Kensington Palace. We were thrilled to learn that we would be presented to Her Royal Highness, Princess Margaret. In keeping with the formal occasion, Pat wore a blue floral dress with a matching large hat and I wore my gray suit. We left Stockport by train for London, arriving at Euston station early enough for us to walk across central London to Kensington Palace. Little did we realize how far it was! We were going to be late. We tried hailing a cab but none would stop; rushing quickly, we arrived on time, but hot and flushed from our exertions. We spent the next hour being instructed on how to line up for the reception, how to bow and curtsey and especially how we were not to initiate conversation with Her Royal Highness. The reception and presentations were rather boring because most of the time we stood around waiting to be personally introduced to the Princess. However, the presentation went well with the exception of some American teachers who felt that they deserved the right to say "Hi!" to the Princess. After the introductions we were offered refreshments. The only other people we knew there were the Stewarts, who had also come down from Ilkley.

On our return to Ilkley we received a letter from Doug Baker, my Technical Director in Picton, who wrote that he and his wife, Roxie, were coming to England for a short holiday in early July. We invited them to stay with us until the English school year ended in July, following which we would tour parts of the south of England.

Doug and Roxie arrived in Manchester and stayed with Nell while they toured Stockport. They arrived in Ilkley a few days before my school year ended and, after unpacking his case, Doug presented me with a tin of twenty-five El Producto cigars! I had not smoked since February following a heavy cold, but that did not stop Doug and me smoking all those cigars during their visit. Unfortunately, my nicotine cravings were aroused, and I went back to smoking my pipe.

Prior to leaving Ilkley, we closed up the house, leaving the keys with our next-door neighbour, settled all our accounts, and closed our bank account. We rented a minivan, which was very comfortable and seated all seven of us with sufficient room for our luggage. That summer of 1975 turned out to be one of the hottest and driest on record, with fires breaking out in the countryside. The motorways were still in the early stages of construction and did not traverse the country as extensively as today. For short periods of time we were able to travel quickly on stretches of motorway, only to return to slow two-lane roads as the motorway ended.

We visited Devon and Cornwall, stopping at many of the usual tourist locations — Exeter, Lyme Regis, Tintagel, Polperro, Lands End, Linton, Lynmouth and Newquay. After an enjoyable holiday trip, we said farewell to Doug and Roxie at Manchester Airport. In the following days, before departing for Canada, we visited with Pat's mother and my mother in Stockport to say our good-byes.

We stepped off the plane in Toronto, tired from the long journey, but happy to be on our way home to Picton.

Chapter 23

A TEMPORARY TEACHER'S DILEMMA

A DJUSTING TO LIFE IN small-town Yorkshire is certainly different from living in small-town Picton, Ontario. However, we were to learn that the Reid family experienced many more problems than we had faced during our year on international exchange.

Financially, it was a disaster for Dennis. His teaching salary from his English school board was deposited directly into C.I.B.C. in Picton. During 1974 and into 1975, the rate of exchange between the English pound and the Canadian dollar steadily dropped from $2.00 to a low of $1.40 to the pound (£). To supplement a foreign teacher's salary, every Canadian teacher was required to give his exchange teacher $500.00 to help offset the cost of living. Adding to Dennis's financial problems was that his wife, Stella, could not obtain employment because they were only visitors to Canada. However, we did learn that Stella eventually worked a part-time job, which helped to supplement their income.

The high school staff went out of its way to assist the Reids. As the weather turned colder, many staff members donated suitable winter clothing for the family because the Reids hadn't anticipated the extreme cold weather of a Canadian winter. At Christmas, the staff collected $750.00, which they donated to the family. We learned that Dennis and Stella made very few friends, preferring to keep to themselves. Perhaps they could not afford to spend money on socializing. Perhaps, like us, they were homesick.

The Technical Department staff comprised of a group of highly qualified and dedicated teachers, who liked to play tricks on each other.

Dennis, who was somewhat aloof, experienced a lot of discomfort when he became the butt of many of these tricks. Each day, when Dennis came into the department staff room, he would place his overshoes at the side of the fridge and then put his lunch in the fridge. After he left for his class, someone would stick his overshoes in the fridge, and in time, thinking it was a crazy Canadian custom, he started putting them there himself. On occasion, a staff member would partially stuff his overshoes with paper and then sit back watching Dennis struggling to get them on. He never understood their sense of humour so they soon grew tired of trying to get him to lighten up. Dennis was too stiff upper-lipped. Had he joined in with them, he would have found a warm, welcoming group.

Dennis must have thought he had died and gone to heaven when he walked into his classroom! Unlike the shortage of equipment and supplies that I had in Leeds, he had everything at his disposal. Each workstation was equipped with all the required drafting equipment. Paper supplies and textbooks for junior and senior classes were plentiful. But he reverted to his old habit. Each time he prepared and duplicated work material he demanded the students hand the sheets back at the end of class. To my knowledge, he performed his teaching duties as required, but his rapport with the students was weak.

Every year, during the last ten days of school, the administration conducts daily staff meetings during which each student's work, in every grade and in every subject, is examined. After the final exams had been written and students had gone for the season, each teacher was required to attend these staff meetings and be available for discussion on any changes that the principal might request. It was an administration decree that you had to be there. Dennis decided otherwise.

After completing all his student evaluations and two weeks before the end of the school year, Dennis told Doug Baker, his department head, that he would be leaving to go off on holiday with his family before returning to the U.K. Dennis was told that he could not approve the request; it had to be approved by the principal. Dennis made an appointment to see Paul Byrd, the principal, and told him of his decision to leave early. There was a very heated, angry discussion between the two with accusations of unprofessional conduct flying back and forth. Knowing Paul Byrd, he must have been close to having a heart attack.

Dennis must have won the argument, or decided he had nothing to lose, because two weeks before the end of the school year the Reids set off on the holiday they had planned. They might well have been saving their money throughout the year for this holiday as they left on a long journey. They drove off in our old family car traveling across to Vancouver, down to San Francisco, across the southern states to the eastern seaboard and back north into Ontario. Amazingly, they had only one problem with the car in having to replace a tire, and the journey was twelve thousand miles long!

We never did see the Reids; they left for England before we returned to Canada and although we wrote to them, we never got a reply. In our correspondence with friends we had made at West Leeds, we were told that Dennis never talked about his experiences at P.E.C.I.

Two years after Dennis returned to England, we were informed that he had left teaching to return to work.

Chapter 24

WASTED YEARS

THE DECREASING STUDENT POPULATION and the Ontario Provincial Government budget cut, as far back as the early seventies, concerned all teaching staffs, but none more than technical teachers. The Ministry of Education for Ontario made serious changes in requirements for high school graduation, which from a political standpoint, were based upon cost-effectiveness. By the late nineties, these changes affected the chances of students getting potential apprenticeship placement in business and industry.

In 1972, the Ministry of Education for Ontario presented the Hall-Dennis Report in which major changes to the curriculum were to be incorporated at the elementary school level. This report stated that students should accept responsibility for their education by allowing them to learn at their own speed, and that the structured walls of the school to be replaced with an open-area concept.

How anyone believed that students would actually read and write and do arithmetic only when they felt ready to learn was beyond reason. All students need defined directions, and one could feel concerned for elementary teachers who were expected to educate students in an environment of organized chaos in an open-area classroom. Elementary students were to be taught in areas divided only by lightweight movable screens separating one class from the next. Students who wanted to learn could not concentrate; those who didn't want to learn had a great excuse not too!

The high school teaching and learning processes were severely affected by the Hall-Dennis Report as students moved into Grade 9, their having little understanding of how to meet subject requirements, how to study for required tests, or how to accept the responsibility for their actions. The Hall-Dennis Report was finally withdrawn, but not before this education system failed a whole generation of students.

A noticeable drop in the student population occurred through the seventies and into the eighties; the Collegiate, which once accommodated fifteen hundred students in the mid-sixties, now attracted an enrolment of only twelve hundred with numbers falling each year. Dropouts were increasing, and fewer students were staying in school, finding little space in their required programs for courses in music, art and technical subjects. However, one of the core subjects had to be drawn from the technologies.

Grades 9 and 10 technical programmes — electrical, auto-mechanics, carpentry, drafting, machine shop — were packaged and presented as introductory subject material. Subjects became more hands on in an attempt to expose students to basic knowledge for further study. Students were turned on, and parents were becoming more supportive of the technical programs. We were overcoming the attitude, "They will learn when they are ready."

Technical education, once a male domain, developed courses in such subjects as home design and layout, and basic household repairs for girls in Grades 11 and 12. These courses were aligned to the home and business economics courses in which many of these girls were enrolled. There was never any shortage of candidates among senior girls.

In the past, only a small number of girls had chosen to study drafting, but now, some classes were composed solely of girls. At class period change, I was chasing boys away from their girl friends who were waiting to get into my class! Stools attached to the drafting stations were not designed for those girls who, wearing short skirts, needed to straddle the seat; too often, these skirts slid up their legs. Most of the girls wore jeans or sat sidesaddle, but some deliberately wore skirts to embarrass me. I allowed the students to play music, quietly, during their practical work time, but we had an agreement on what was played; one day we played their music, next day my music. I learned about Credence Clear Water and Led Zeppelin. They got to know Barry Manilow and Barbra Streisand.

At a recent gathering of retired teachers, one of the wives told me that her daughter, a former student of mine who is a banker, had been involved with designing structural changes taking place within her department. The construction engineers were amazed that she was able to suggest possible improvements to the project as well as read blueprints, until she told them of the drafting course she had taken back in the eighties. It made me feel good to know that teaching drafting courses to girls actually paid off. However, major budget cutbacks within the provincial and local budgets forced the cancellation of these girls' courses and other senior technical courses that were becoming too expensive to maintain.

More paperwork and subject justifications were required by the Ministry, which asked teachers to carry out evaluation of all teaching costs through E.R.A.S. (Educational Resources Allocation System). Teachers were requested to analyze each concept, which involved budgeted expenses of their programme, to find if costs could be reduced or shared with other programmes in their department and within the school. Technical department expenditures were under pressure because of the rising costs of equipment, supplies and machine replacement. After all the time and effort spent on the ERAS report, suddenly it was withdrawn. For what reason, I will never know. Could it be because of the regular chanting of "Up ERAS, Up ERAS!" at the start of every staff meeting?

Student population continued to decline and redundancies were applied to eliminate staff. Budgets were tightened, courses were eliminated, educational directions changed, and still we strove to provide the students with the best teaching and course material possible under such stringent conditions.

In the early 1980's, the Ministry of Education for Ontario, preferring not to buy I.B.M. systems, spent thousands of dollars having an offshore computer system developed specifically for schools. The Ministry selected our technical department to field test this new system named ICON. Ron Hotston, our electricity teacher, was asked to examine the capabilities of the hardware, and I was to evaluate the drafting software. The software instructions — two sheets of less than useful information — were sadly lacking in detail and of little use to students. I wrote a software-drafting manual for students, published by McGraw-Hill Ryerson, entitled *Step by Step Through the CAD Tutor*. Ron Hotston became so competent with the hardware that the Ministry would often refer teachers from other schools to ask his advice on problems for which they had no answers. The Ministry requested Ron and me, as a team, to perform workshops on the ICON system, in locations throughout Ontario. However, when the Ministry found that their ICON system was not compatible with commercially available software, they scrapped the project. By the mid-80's, Ontario technical departments, now using I.B.M. systems, moved into Computer Aided Drafting — CAD, and Computer Aided Machining — CAM.

So that I could stay ahead of the students, it became crucial for me to buy a personal computer. Largely from playing video games, many students became more adept than I with their computer skills. However, I was much more familiar with the drafting software. I often read the monthly magazine, *Computer News,* and in one of its issues, a prize of a laptop was being offered to whoever could write the funniest caption for a cartoon picture. I cannot remember what words I proposed, except it contained "bits and bytes." One day after school, Pat told me someone had phoned about a laptop computer. When I phoned back, the editor of the computer magazine told me that my caption had won me the laptop valued at $2,000.00. A year later, I sold it for $1,300.00

I took early retirement in June 1989, and later realized that I had chosen the right time. Since leaving the profession, many changes have taken place in education and especially in technical education. Machine shop, electronics, welding and farm mechanics were closing down. Computers replaced drafting boards. Technical education was surviving in name only on the backs of carpentry, electricity and auto-mechanics.

The proud heritage of the P.E.C.I. Technical Department was gone for good. And to make matters worse, students were now telling teachers that they had rights as to what and how they would learn!

Chapter 25

WE NEVER KNOW WHEN LIFE WILL END —
PART ONE

I AM PROUD THAT I chose Canada to be my home, especially on July 1, when I participate in our village Canada Day Parade. Many residents of our retirement community get involved in the parade either in marching, or handing out candy to the children, or riding on a flatbed trailer decorated to celebrate Canada's birthday. It is a day to be happy; yet it is a day to be sad. On that day in 1993, after thirty-five years of happy marriage, Patricia died.

Patricia's health problems began long before I knew her. She was a sickly child, who lost much time at school, and who suffered bronchial complications from rheumatic fever. At age eleven, she underwent surgery to remove part of a lung. She was susceptible to colds and chills and her parents made sure she did not physically overtax herself. While growing up, she was able to lead a normal life, as long as she did not exert herself or to get too tired. I met Pat when she was just seventeen years old — pretty, shy and quiet — and showing no evidence of her physical limitations.

Some years after we married, she developed rheumatoid arthritis. Gradually, her condition worsened; she suffered much pain while her fingers and toes slowly grew deformed. On many nights, I could hear her quietly crying from the pain. I only wish that I could have been more supportive.

She had been prescribed every available arthritis drug, and she often said that she was surprised she didn't rattle from all the pills she was swallowing! Her specialist recommended corrective surgery to straighten her fingers. The operation was performed at Wellesley Hospital, Toronto, and following the successful surgery, she no longer tried to hide her hands.

For many years she wore orthopaedic shoes to ease the pain in her toes and joints. Because of the successful operation on her hands the previous year, her specialist recommended corrective surgery on her feet. In October, we went to Toronto for her surgical pre-op tests. During the tests, the doctors discovered the level of oxygen in Pat's blood was so low that the strain on her heart might precipitate her having a heart attack. They were surprised that she still walked around under such conditions and immediately placed her on oxygen support. They also told her that she would need to sleep with a steady flow of oxygen. She was utterly demoralized.

It was now obvious that I needed to be readily available to help Pat with her medical problems. I decided to pursue early retirement at the end of that school year. The Teacher's Federation had extended a three-year option allowing teachers who were more than fifty-five and who had taught for at least ten years, an early retirement. In addition, their pensions would not be penalized.

Unable to accept having to wear an oxygen supply for the rest of her life, Pat went into a deep depression, shutting everyone out. She said people would say that she was a freak; her friends would be overly sympathetic, or worse — ignore her. I stood by, feeling helpless. I seriously thought that Pat was considering taking her own life. After much time and counselling with the Ontario Lung Association, she accepted that she could still lead an active life while living with oxygen dependency.

We wanted to take longer journeys than just driving around the local area. We would need to travel with an oxygen supply and we were informed that many supply locations existed across North America. No matter where we went, arrangements could be made for us to replenish the supply of oxygen. Since we had never been to the Maritimes, we decided to drive to Nova Scotia. We were amazed at the number of locations available for oxygen supply along the route we had planned, and arrangements were made to change oxygen tanks as we needed them. We drove a small car at that time, but we were able to place the oxygen tank in the back seat. We enjoyed our travels through Quebec, New Brunswick and into Nova Scotia as we explored the Cabot Trail, Cape Breton and P.E.I. We saw that we could indeed live life to the fullest, even while dragging around oxygen tanks. As the weeks and months passed, the doctor prescribed an increase in the flow rate of oxygen. It soon became evident that Pat would have future difficulties with her breathing

We withdrew some of our savings and bought a minivan which gave us more space for oxygen tanks and supplies; since we were now able to take extra supply tanks with us we did not have to be restricted to short hops between oxygen stops. Distance was no problem, so we decided to visit the one place Pat had always wanted to visit since she had agreed to emigrate to Canada—British Columbia.

Our western summer trip took us through Ontario along the spectacular shoreline of Lake Superior and across the Prairies where the flat landscape allowed us to see city skylines almost a day before we reached them. Driving through the mountains of British Columbia and over to Vancouver Island by ferry, we were taken aback by the majesty of nature in that part of Canada. On our return journey, we stopped in the Okanagan Valley of B.C. and visited a retirement park, similar to the one in which I now live. We were so moved by the experience that we talked about moving to B.C.

Pat often spent time in the hospital to rest and to readjust to the change in the oxygen supply rate. I know she sometimes asked her doctor to place her in the hospital so that I could get some rest. However, I accepted the need to do extra housework, or cook the meals, or push Pat around in her wheel chair.

She asked her doctor to tell her the truth about her condition and how long she might have left to live; his prognosis was that she had from one to three years. To my astonishment, Pat showed no surprise. There was no weeping or sadness. Convincing me that it could be sooner rather than later, she asked me to help her in planning her funeral arrangements and in preparing her will. Pat said that when she was gone I was not to sit around and grieve, and that I was to get on with my life. We were even able to smile when she told me I should get married again, ... "but you must promise you won't marry a younger woman!"

How Pat could be so brave in the face of her medical future, I will never know. But she was to be faced with another difficult setback.

WE NEVER KNOW WHEN LIFE WILL END —
PART TWO

O NE NIGHT, PAT WOKE me up saying she could smell oil. My sense of smell was not as sharp as hers, so I got up and went down to the recreation room to investigate. I stepped off the bottom step and onto the basement floor, into a pool of oil! The fuel tank had been filled the previous day. Knowing the fumes would be harmful to Pat's breathing, I quickly returned to the bedroom and asked her to dress so I could get her out onto the porch and out into the fresh air. I returned to survey the damage and found the oil had not only covered the floor, saturating the carpet, but also had flowed across into the utility room.

At 7:00 a.m., I contacted the house insurance company, which quickly arranged to dispatch a clean-up specialist; an insurance adjuster would be there to see me before 9:00 a.m. All this time, Pat had been sitting outside on the porch getting very cold. I phoned our friends, Peter and Hilary, explaining the situation and they immediately asked me to bring Pat to their house. After leaving her there, I returned home to meet with the cleaning company and the insurance adjuster. At 8:00 a.m. the clean-up crew arrived, ready to survey the site and to decide how they would tackle the problem. The insurance adjuster came to evaluate the situation and, after talking with the cleaners, told me that the damage was covered by our insurance and all would be taken care of. He said it could be several weeks before the work was completed so we would need alternative accommodation, but I asked him to delay any decision on accommodation until I had talked with Pat.

At first, Pat was upset with this news. I explained that everything was under control and that workers had already begun to clear up the mess. I told her that it could be several weeks before we could return to the house, and that the insurance company would cover the costs of accommodation. Peter and Hilary invited us to stay in the granny suite that they had built as part of their house. We accepted their generous offer.

The cleaning crew explained that while the oil was flooding the floor, the walls and furniture had acted like wicks soaking up the oil. The wall coverings had to be removed back to the bare block work. Even the lower course of concrete blocks had absorbed the oil. I was told everything in the house would have to be cleaned — clothing, curtains and all upstairs upholstery — because the oil fumes would permeate the material. We had nothing but praise for our insurance company and the work done by the company. As promised, several weeks later we returned to the house, which was now free of oil fumes and safe for Pat to live in. During the reconstruction, we installed a gas central heating system. When the final bill came in, the cost to repair the damage was more than $30,000.00.

A few weeks after we had returned to live in the house, Pat told me she could still smell oil. I was so concerned for her breathing that I invited several friends to come over, quietly asking them without Pat's knowledge, if they could smell oil. No one could and I wondered if the problem was psychological. Pat said she wanted us to sell the house and leave as quickly as possible. I was rather upset after all we had gone through, but I agreed that we put the house on the market.

We found that a retirement park community, similar to the one we had visited in B.C. was being built in the village of Wellington, just a few miles from where we presently lived. In December, we visited the site and decided to build a house there. The lot we chose was located close to the recreation centre, which also overlooked the activities' areas — lawn bowling, shuffleboard and tennis. From the deck of our house, Pat would be able to watch residents at play, although she would be unable to participate. After signing an agreement to build the house, construction began in February with a completion date of mid-June. We planned to move to Wellington on July 1, 1993.

Throughout the winter and spring, Pat returned to the hospital several times. The oxygen flow, which had started at one litre a minute three years ago, was now up to nine litres a minute. Whenever I visited Pat while she was in the hospital, we would discuss any changes we should make in the new house. The plan required an open-area design because Pat would be confined to a wheel chair. Although we were excited about our new house, we were also excited to learn that our eldest son, Paul, and his wife Susan, were expecting a baby in early June.

In May, we had a phone call from my sister Audrey, who told us that she and Alban had received a free trip to New York through a promotion, which was included in the purchase of their new vacuum cleaner. Although the trip would be short, they looked forward to visiting with us and seeing the new house. A few days after Audrey and Alban arrived in Picton, our granddaughter, Lauren, was born on June 3. Together with Pat, we all drove to Ottawa to see the baby. When Pat held Lauren in her arms, I think for a brief moment in time, she felt free of her illness. I am convinced she fought to live long enough to see her grandchild.

During her stay, Audrey told me that my nephew was getting married in England in August 1994, and she hoped we would be able to come for the wedding. I quietly said that I doubted that we would be able to make the trip, but that if anything happened to Pat in the meantime, I promised I would come for the wedding. She said, "I hope I don't see you."

Shortly after Audrey and Alban returned to England, Pat was admitted to Kingston General. On June 30, 2003 at 6:00 p.m., I received a call from the Kingston hospital telling me she had slipped into a coma. When I arrived at the hospital, they told me there was little hope she would survive the night. I was prepared to stay as long as it took, which I hoped would be forever. Pat had never deserved to suffer as she had throughout the years, but I knew it would be a release from her pain for her to let go.

As she lay in a coma, I talked to her, telling her all the things I should have told her over the years. I told her very personal things that belonged only to the two of us. I believe that Pat could hear me, since I had heard that people in a coma are able hear what is being said to them. Constantly, throughout the night, the nurse would come into the room to monitor Pat's condition. She told me she was slipping away, slowly but inevitably. Eight hours after I had arrived, I asked the nurse to remove Pat's cannula, because I believed she would want to pass from this life without wearing the burden she had accepted for the last four years. At 3:00 a.m. Pat died.

It was like walking in a dream, leaving the hospital. Outside it was quiet, still and lonely, and as I drove home from Kingston along the road that Pat and I had travelled together so many times, I remember the radio station playing Kenny Rogers "Through the Years," and every word of the song brought into focus the life that Pat and I had shared for close to thirty-four years.

I stopped off at the house in Picton, now emptied, the furniture having all been moved to the new house the previous day. As I walked from room to room, I checked to see what might have been left behind, but also hoping to sense Pat's spirit. Before leaving the house for the last time, I phoned the funeral home and told the director that Pat had died and asked him to carry out her last wishes. I left a house, which had seen too much suffering and frustration, but I took all the love and memories with me to Wellington.

It was July 1, 1993, Canada's birthday. The day that Patricia died

Chapter 26

RESTARTING MY LIFE

FOLLOWING PAT'S DEATH, I was overwhelmed by sorrow and anger, unable to believe that after almost forty years I was now alone. I was especially angry with God for not helping to ease her pain because Pat should not have suffered as she had, having always put other people's concerns before her own. I would fall asleep crying and searching for answers to my questions of why she had to die. I was not able to come up with answers.

Although it was uncomfortable to do so, Pat and I had prepared her funeral arrangements with the local director several months before she died. Those decisions were of great help to me during the days immediately following her death. News of Pat's death spread quickly. The family joined me for the visitation on July 3, as did our many friends and neighbours who came to express their condolences. Paul, Michael and Steven helped me to bear up during this emotionally draining time. The following week, Pat's ashes were interred in Cherry Valley Cemetery at a private family gathering.

Upon waking up early every morning, my thoughts in turmoil, I tried making decisions about my future life. I was torn between either remaining in Wellington, or returning to England. My sons had grown up in the County, I had lived here most of my life and Pat was buried here. Should I stay or go? I was helped by a neighbour who had recently lost his wife and in discussing together our feelings and concerns about our present situations I was finally able, by weighing both options, to make a decision. I decided to remain in Wellington. Then Fate stepped in and helped to confirm my decision.

A new fridge and stove were due to be delivered to my house in Wellington on the Lake and I wanted to dispose of the used units. A neighbour suggested that I phone the local United Church minister to ask if his church accepted such items to be passed on to needy families. He accepted my offer and before we ended the conversation, I asked if I could attend his church service on Sunday, explaining that I was a baptized Anglican. He replied by saying that everyone was welcome at the United Church of Canada.

The following Sunday, I attended church. Several times during the service my eyes welled up as my thoughts turned to Pat. The solemnity of the recessional hymn moved me to tears and I sat quietly in the pew waiting for everyone to leave. As I rose to go, a lady approached me saying she was very pleased that I had earlier visited Tara Hall and paid the costs of the bed and breakfast for "my relatives" who had stayed overnight! I very politely told her that she had confused me with someone else, to which she asked, "Aren't you Peter Worthington?" "No," I said. "My name is Roy Goostrey." She was somewhat embarrassed, but she introduced herself as Elaine, and invited me to meet her sister who was waiting for her outside the church door. Elaine introduced me to Yvonne, a tall, slim blonde wearing large dark sunglasses and a bright yellow dress. I was invited to visit Tara Hall, where Elaine and her husband ran a B&B, later that afternoon, but I declined because I had planned to play golf in Picton. She then asked if I would at least drop by for a drink on my return home. Politely, I answered, "I will see."

Knowing that I would be spending the evening alone, I had rented a video "The Last of the Mohicans." As I was driving back into Wellington, I suddenly remembered that I had said I would stop at Tara Hall, so I felt obligated to visit. Elaine invited me in and introduced me to her husband Richard, explaining to him, "He looks like Peter Worthington, doesn't he?" Peter Worthington, who lives close to Wellington, is a well-known journalist and contributor to several National newspapers. As we chatted over drinks, Yvonne joined us. I learned that Yvonne, a retired teacher from Winnipeg, was assisting Elaine and Richard with their new business. I was invited to stay for supper and later that evening, as I excused myself to leave, I extended an invitation to Yvonne to come and see my new house and also to watch the video. She accepted my offer.

We played the video, but kept stopping it to chat; we were both so interested in what the other had to say. I learned that Yvonne, upon retirement from teaching, had enrolled at the University of Winnipeg to study toward completion of an M.A. degree. But she had fallen in love with Wellington and on impulse had just bought a house on Main Street. Soon, she was to return to Winnipeg to pack her furniture for removal to Wellington. Later that night, after driving Yvonne back to Tara Hall, I thought about our discussions during the evening, and I could not believe that someone could be so genuinely interested in what I had to say. For the first time in many days I slept well because I sensed a change in the direction of my life was about to take place.

The following morning I phoned Yvonne and asked her, "How impulsive are you?" "Try me!" she said. Much to her delight, I presented her with a single carnation when I arrived on her doorstep at 11:30 a.m.. As we drove the County roads, I told her about the history of the Loyalists who settled the area following the American Revolution. We drove through Picton, along the Glenora Road to Lake on the Mountain. We stopped for lunch at the Duke of North Marysburg Pub in Waupoos, and then drove to the Sandbanks Provincial Park, a popular tourist area, where we walked on Outlet Beach. We returned to my house for supper and because Yvonne had said that she liked Kraft Dinners, we ate macaroni and cheese before I took her back to Tara Hall. Yvonne left for Winnipeg the next day.

I kept in contact with Yvonne during the time she was in Winnipeg. Our local florist thought I was crazy when I asked her to send, "one red rose" to Winnipeg. Her sister told me Yvonne's birthday was in September. I planned to give her a special gift. My sister sent me the sound track of the show "Miss Siagon", which I often played while driving alone. The show was playing at the Prince of Wales Theater in Toronto until October. I booked tickets for the last weekend in September. At the end of August, Yvonne arrived back from Winnipeg to begin her new life in Wellington where she was more than content to settle into her new house (the Doll's House) on Main Street.

As Yvonne's birthday approached, I told her of my gift and invited her not only to see "Miss Saigon," but also to spend a few days driving south through Pennsylvania and Virginia. In late October, we drove to Scarborough, and then took the train into downtown Toronto. After attending the performance, we returned to Union Station. That night held a special significance for the city of Toronto in that their team, the Blue Jays, had won the World Series Baseball Championship. Afraid that we might miss our train, we fought our way though throngs of cheering crowds gathered along the streets. Fortunately, we arrived on time to catch the train.

The next day, we drove into the USA down into Virginia. There among the brilliant fall colours of the landscape, we toured the Blue Ridge Mountains and the Shenandoah Valley. Many times I had visited the Civil War sites in the area, especially Gettysburg, and since Yvonne had never been there we stayed on for a few days. After returning to Wellington, I questioned my emotions and reflected on the time Yvonne and I had shared together. I knew that she was a very special lady.

I hoped that this was the start of a relationship that would only strengthen with time.

Chapter 27

TOWARD THE FUTURE

A WARM, LOVING RELATIONSHIP IS based upon a solid foundation of having mutual respect for one another and being able to accept the other's point of view in open and honest communication. From the first day we met, and as we spent more time together, it was becoming increasingly evident that Yvonne and I were developing a serious relationship.

We did crazy things — getting caught in the pouring rain visiting the Peterborough Lift Locks, getting lost while hiking in Algonquin Park, driving miles to see the Petroglyphs — sacred Indian writings and drawings — and arriving to find the gates of the park had closed, and still we laughed. Often, while driving around the County, we stopped the car to eat a "ditch picnic," and at night, we sometimes lay down on the deck at my house trying to count the myriad of stars. They were zany times, but they were warm and sincere.

Yvonne had been introduced to my oldest son Paul, and his wife Sue, when we visited them in Ottawa. She was yet to meet Michael and Steven. One evening, I arranged with them to meet for dinner in Belleville where Yvonne received a warm and loving welcome from the boys. The week before my sixtieth birthday, Paul phoned to say that they would be coming to visit me on that day and I told him that we had been invited to Yvonne's house for coffee and birthday cake after dinner. Imagine my delight when we arrived to find that she had arranged a surprise birthday gathering for my family and friends. I had been waiting for a suitable time to propose marriage and that time had now arrived.

For my birthday gift, Yvonne had booked us to stay for the weekend at our favourite getaway location, the Riveredge Hotel in beautiful Alexandria Bay, New York. During the time I had known Yvonne, I had written a number of poems, some of which she had read, but not the one I had just written which ended with a proposal of marriage! Following dinner that night, I nervously reached into my pocket for the poem and with shaking hands tried to remain calm while squinting to read the small print. I reached for my glasses but I had left them in the room! Somehow, I managed to contain the moment until we returned to our room. While it took some moments for Yvonne to fully realize the intent of the poem, she did make me very happy by accepting my proposal.

Over the next few weeks, we talked of little else but our wedding plans. Yvonne wanted me to meet her family and to inform them personally of our upcoming wedding. In May, we left for a five-week round trip from Ontario to Vancouver Island with stops in Winnipeg, Brandon, Regina, Edmonton, Jasper and Vancouver. Yvonne's daughter, Dreena, and her family lived in Vancouver.

Following Pat's death, I had arranged to visit England in August 1994 to attend my nephew Neil's wedding. Even though we had planned our wedding to take place in September, Yvonne told me that I should continue with my plans. She would complete the arrangements for our wedding while I was abroad.

In early August, I flew to England for a three-week visit.

Chapter 28

THE LATER YEARS – A CONCLUSION

BUGLE BOY MEMORIES, WHICH span seventy–five years, reflect some of my experiences both before and after emigrating to Canada from England. Since Yvonne and I married fifteen years ago, we have traveled extensively, been actively involved in our retirement community and watched our families grow. As I reach the end of these memoirs, I include a brief overview of those last few years.

After attending my nephew's wedding in England in 1994, I returned to Wellington to find that Yvonne had completed the plans for our wedding to be held on September 24. We were thrilled that her daughter, Dreena, was coming from Vancouver to be her matron of honour. We both attended the United Church in Wellington and Yvonne, who is from a Ukrainian family and has an Orthodox religious background, arranged with the minister to perform a ceremony including aspects from both rituals.

We extended an invitation to the whole village to join in the celebration of our marriage and, following the ceremony, to attend a luncheon in the church hall. Later that evening, we continued our celebrations by inviting friends and neighbours to attend our wedding dinner and dance held at the Recreation Center at Wellington on the Lake. We honeymooned in Eastern Canada, first stopping in Quebec City to immerse ourselves in the history and architecture of the old city. Then we drove to New Brunswick, along the Cabot trail in Nova Scotia and then to Prince Edward Island before returning to Ontario by way of Gaspe Bay and the St. Lawrence Seaway.

That winter, we spent two months in a rented house in Florida. We soon got caught up in the Snowbird culture and in 1998, we bought a house in a gated community in Port Charlotte. We spent every winter there until we sold it in 2004, just before Hurricane Charlie blew in to destroy the park. We discussed the possibility of spending the winter of 2005 in Dorset on the south coast of England, so we asked our friends, John and Maureen, to search for a cottage rental. They found April Cottage, a modern house whose facade blended with the seventeenth-century houses in the small village of Upwey. This was to be the first of several visits to the Weymouth area especially meaningful to Yvonne as a retired English teacher. Dorchester and Weymouth were the settings for the many novels and poetry written by the author, Thomas Hardy. His travels took him all around the county, and he often frequented our local pub down the street. We broadened our winter experiences by spending one winter in an historic cottage in Looe, Cornwall and another winter in Albufeira in Portugal.

During the summer, we both became involved in many activities at Wellington on the Lake. Yvonne was involved in line dancing, tap-dancing, clogging, ladies' snooker and aerobics. I played tennis, which I had last played as a teenager, and I became a lawn bowler, even though I had always associated lawn bowling with old men. When I was a kid, I remember watching them on the bowling greens, smoking their pipes, or sucking on their cigs, or taking a swig from their pints of beer before sending the bowl on a curving path across the crown of a lawn-bowling green. We both took active roles in the amateur shows our community produced as we acted, sang and danced to entertain our neighbours. I cannot remember where all that time went, but there never seemed to be enough of it.

Throughout the years, my family continued to grow and mature as both my younger sons married and raised families of their own. I now have seven much-loved grandchildren, all of whom play an important part in my life. So that they would know of their background, I gave each family member a copy of my original memoirs entitled, *The Road Less Traveled*, which I wrote in 2000. Having read that book, several of my friends from immigrant backgrounds recognized the similarities between their experiences and mine, thus prompting me to rewrite the book for a wider audience.

If you find reminders of days gone by as they did, then this book has been worth the effort taken to bring it to publication.